six sessions

start>

Becoming a Good Samaritan

Participant's Guide

MICHAEL SEATON with *Ashley Wiersma*

ZONDERVAN®   **World Vision**
Building a better world for children

ZONDERVAN.com/
AUTHOR**TRACKER**
follow your favorite authors

ZONDERVAN

Start Becoming a Good Samaritan Participant's Guide
Copyright © 2009 by Michael Seaton

Requests for information should be addressed to:

Zondervan, *Grand Rapids, Michigan 49530*

ISBN 978-0-310-28504-5

Action-Item Research Lead: Shannon Ford

World Vision Liaison: Kim Browne

Published in association with the literary agency of Alive Communications, Inc., 7680 Goddard Street, Suite 200, Colorado Springs, CO 80920. www.alivecommunications.com

Cover photography: Jeff Casemier
Interior design: Ben Fetterley

Printed in the United States of America

10 11 12 13 14 15 /DCI/ 28 27 26 25 24 23 22 21 20 19 18 17 16 15 14 13 12 11 10 9 8 7 6 5 4

Contents

People of the Possible and a Gospel Devoid of Holes[1]

Rich Stearns, President, World Vision U.S.

There's a well-known passage in Matthew 25 that describes a day when the Son of Man will come in his glory with all the angels in tow, and with all the nations gathered before him, he will separate the people one from another as a shepherd separates the sheep from the goats. Interestingly, the criterion for dividing them is *not* that the "sheep" confessed faith in Christ while the "goats" did not. It's that the sheep acted in tangible and loving ways toward the poor, the sick, the imprisoned, and the vulnerable, while the goats, as it turns out, did not.

I know you're not supposed to rewrite Scripture, but every time I come across that sheep-versus-goats text, I find myself mentally adapting the verses for an affluent, twenty-first century audience:

> *For I was hungry, while you had all you needed.*
> *I was thirsty, but you drank bottled water.*
> *I was a stranger, and you wanted me deported.*
> *I needed clothes, but you needed more clothes.*
> *I was sick, and you pointed out the behaviors that led to my sickness.*
> *I was in prison, and you said I was getting what I deserved.*

— RESV (Richard E. Stearns Version)

Either way you read it, God has clear expectations for those who choose to follow him. While we are not saved by piling up enough good works to try to satisfy our heavenly Father, if we take Christ at his word, then we know that an authentic and genuine commitment to him simply *must* carry with it demonstrable evidence of a transformed life; otherwise we have subscribed to a gospel with a giant hole in it. In other words, our faith is marked not only by a personal and transforming relationship with God, but also by a *public* and *transforming* relationship with the world. This is the "whole gospel" I believe Christ intends for us to live by and to communicate to a broken and needy world.

Eleven years ago I was given the opportunity to embrace the whole gospel when World Vision invited me to leave my job as a corporate CEO and become its U.S. president. I felt compelled to pursue such an unparalleled opportunity to demonstrate the love of Christ to the poor — my passion since the day I committed my life to Christ in my twenties. I'd always wanted nothing more than to join God in building his coming kingdom — a kingdom in which the poor would be helped, the downtrodden would be lifted up, human dignity would be restored, oppression would be challenged, and biblical justice would be proclaimed.

But how could I — just one fallen man — help usher in such massive change?

Perhaps you too can relate. You see grave societal injustices and ills all around, and you wonder how they could possibly get fixed. Either you could become so overwhelmed by the sheer magnitude of the challenges that you turn away, hopeless, convinced that nothing you do will ever make a difference. Or you could dive in with naive enthusiasm, underestimating the problems, only to burn out from discouragement after the first few setbacks. But you know as well as I do that neither of these approaches is very useful. The pessimist sees only obstacles; the optimist sees only opportunities. But it's the *realist* who sees the possibilities between the two. And that's who you and I must be: people of the possible.

I've seen the hungry fed and people taught to fish and farm. I've watched wells being drilled and cisterns being built — the thirsty given water. I have seen the sick healed, the lame walk, and the blind given back their sight. I have met refugees who have been resettled, disaster victims who've been restored, and captives who have been released. I've seen widows comforted, orphans cared for, children freed from slavery and abuse, schools built, clinics opened, babies vaccinated, loans lifting the poor out of poverty — I've witnessed these things with my own eyes. But even greater than these, I have seen the gaze of Christ staring back at me through the eyes of the poor, and the love of Christ demonstrated to them through the lives and deeds of his faithful servants. Best of all, I've watched them find new life in the One who created them. I have been an eyewitness to these things — to this amazing, full gospel transforming the most broken of lives and flooding the darkest of places with the radiant light of hope. I know these things are possible. And we must be people of the possible.

"I tell you the truth," Jesus says in Matthew 17:20, "if you have faith as small as a mustard seed, you can say to this mountain, 'Move from here to there' and it will move. Nothing will be impossible for you." I used to read that verse and think that it was an exaggeration, that Jesus was just trying to make a point about the power of faith. But recently I came to view it in a different light. What if Jesus meant for millions of his followers each to put his or her faith into action by grabbing a shovel and challenging the mountain one shovelful at a time? Then *any* mountain would be moved, even the peaks of Poverty, Hunger, and Injustice — if we had enough people out there "shoveling."

These days I find myself wondering what would happen if the world's two billion Christians instantly became *possibility-minded* and took seriously Christ's call to transform our world — if we actually picked up our shovels and worked to move some dirt. Two thousand years ago, twelve men so empowered *did* move mountains. I believe it can happen again, and I have a hunch it will start with us.

In the end, God doesn't require us to be superstars. He simply calls us to be faithful to the things he has given us to do — praying, loving, serving, giving, forgiving, healing, and caring — doing "small things," as Mother Teresa once said, "with great love." *This* is the whole of the gospel. And if we each embrace it, we will see the world we live in change.

How to Use This Guide

Thanks for choosing to **start>**! This participant's guide was designed to accompany the *start> Becoming a Good Samaritan* DVD, which includes a helpful leader's guide to orient you to the curriculum. Our hope is that you will rally a few of your friends or family members in the context of a small group at church or simply around a table at your local coffee shop and work through each of the six sessions in turn. The sessions are brief—each takes about an hour—and can be completed at the pace of your choosing—weekly, biweekly, monthly, or whatever works best for you.

You'll notice that each session contains two major sections: "Group Interaction" and "Personal Reflection." Plan to complete the entire Group Interaction portion with your other group members according to the time designations noted beside each session subheading; then, if a particular session piques your interest, work through the three-part Personal Reflection portion between group meetings on your own. Here's how the group time breaks out:

- Get Connected (1 minute)—read a brief overview of the session content

- Know Your Neighbor (2 minutes)—air your current beliefs or assumptions about the topic

- Give Your Heart and Mind to God (1 minute)—ask for God's presence and guidance as you begin

- Learn Together (30 minutes)—view the session video segment on the DVD

- Discuss "Becoming a Good Samaritan" (20 minutes)*—talk about ideas and insights that are sparked by the DVD content

- Now Is the Time (5 minutes)*—try your hand at putting your faith in action

- Close with Prayer (1 minute)—dismiss your group time

Ready to get started? All you need is a few friends, a TV or computer with DVD capability, a Bible, a pen, and this guide. To connect with others who are working to put their faith into action, visit juststart.org. There you'll find speaker bios, video extras, **start>** church campaign resources, and more. The Good Samaritan journey is the path God intends for *all* of his followers to walk. We are thrilled that you've agreed to taking the first step.

---

* Sessions 4 and 6 have 15 minutes allotted for group discussion and 10 minutes allotted for the "Now Is the Time" activity.

1

Becoming a Good Samaritan
Who Is My Neighbor?

> "I can neither meet the needs of everyone in the world nor take anyone's needs lightly."
>
> — Lynne Hybels, author, speaker, and activist

start> Group Interaction

> Get Connected   1 minute

Have someone in the group read aloud this brief description of the session theme.

A recent article in *Good* magazine endeavored to sum up the state of planet Earth. What was not necessarily inspiring were details about the challenges presently faced: a tumbling economy, ongoing war, threats of still-daunting ills like disease and hunger and poverty. But what did carry hope was the conclusion the author drew: "The global problems are larger than before," he wrote, "but our capacity to meet them is larger still."[1]

The local church — comprised of people who love God just like you do — is capable of doing what no other band of brothers and sisters can do: unite with love and passion to help bring reconciliation to every heart, soul, and corner of the world.

In this opening session you are invited to explore what it means to move from creed (what you believe) to deed (how those beliefs get acted out) on behalf of those in need around you. If every man, woman, and child who claims the name of Jesus Christ will join the fight against today's biggest threats to the fully reconciled world God dreams of, the world indeed will change. Your actions matter. Your choices matter. Choose today to **start>**.

> Know Your Neighbor   2 minutes

Using one or two words, share your current beliefs or assumptions about the session theme.

Why aren't there more "Good Samaritans" in the world today?

"In everything I did, I showed you that by this kind of hard work we must help the weak, remembering the words the Lord Jesus himself said: 'It is more blessed to give than to receive.'"

— Acts 20:35

> Give Your Heart and Mind to God   1 minute

Before the Good Samaritan in Luke 10 could *act* well, he first had to *see* well. As you prepare your mind and heart for session 1, open in prayer, asking God for eyes to *really see* the people in need where you live. Who are they? What is life like for them? What are their spiritual needs, in addition to those in the physical realm? What resources do you already possess that could help meet a need today? Thank God for giving you eyes that can see, hands that can serve, and a heart that can beat fast for the things that bring him joy.

> Learn Together   30 minutes

If you'd like to take a few notes as you watch the session 1 video segment, use the space below.

> Discuss "Becoming a Good Samaritan"   20 minutes

You may not have time to discuss all of the questions in this section — that's okay! Cover as many as you can, thoughtfully, thoroughly, and with great attentiveness.

1. As you listened to Eugene Peterson recount the parable of the Good Samaritan, what words, phrases, or ideas struck you?

2. In Peterson's transliteration, *The Message*, Luke 10:27 reads this way: "Love the Lord your God with all your passion and prayer and muscle

and intelligence — and … love your neighbor as well as you do yourself." When have you observed Christ-followers you know "loving the
Lord their God" with *each* of the following aspects of their lives? For
example, maybe your mother is a fierce intercessor (prayer), or your
colleague at work teaches classes on generous living at his church
(intelligence).

Passion

Prayer

Muscle/physical strength

Intelligence

Considering those four aspects, which one most accurately reflects
the way that the Good Samaritan loved God as he served the man in
need? Make your selection below, and then explain your rationale to
the other members of your group.

- Through his passion
- Through his prayer
- Through his physical strength
- Through his intelligence

3. Through which of the four aspects — passion, prayer, muscle, intelligence — do you most often sense the love of God flowing out of your
   own life, and which of the four seems to be the most challenging for

you? Share with your small group the life experiences you've had that help explain your responses.

In your view, why is it so important to God that his followers show love in all four ways? Discuss your thoughts with your group.

4. During the video segment, Jim Wallis said, "It's in the places where you're not supposed to belong that you'll learn the most. It's with the people you were never supposed to meet that you come to understand the world better.… And it's in those people that you really encounter Jesus in a way you never knew him before."

    Think about the form of expression — passion, prayer, physical strength, or intelligence — that is most challenging for you. What fears, assumptions, or obstacles keep you from engaging with people in that particular manner?

5. Real joy is found in real obedience to the commands of Christ. As Miles McPherson said, "You can't enter into the joy of the Lord unless you're faithful to do the things that he said to do."

    If Christ desires that you faithfully do the things that he said to do, then he will equip you to do them. What assurances from God might help you to overcome the fears and obstacles that you face? Record your thoughts in the space below, sharing one or two of them with your group.

6. While it's certainly easier to show God's love through prayer or by keeping things intellectual or theoretical, the call to every Christ-follower is to show up in people's lives in a physical, practical way. You can't "phone in" God's love.

    Foundation for American Renewal director Amy Sherman says this regarding the Good Samaritan:

    > It's not like he stood on the other side of the road and threw canned goods and religious tracts at the guy. He crossed the road. He got up-close and personal. He dirtied his own hands. He tore his own clothing. There was something very relational, very hands-on about his ministry.

    As you consider Sherman's comments, think about a time when you have been blessed by someone's decision to get up-close and personal to meet a need in your life. Describe the experience to your group.

    How would you rank how likely you are to involve yourself firsthand for the sake of meeting another person's need? Place an X on the continuum below, and then explain your position to your small group.

    I tend to keep
    my distance

    My hands are
    always dirty!

> Now Is the Time

This is the most important part of the session — how your small group will put faith into action. Make each other accountable for starting today!

In the spirit of getting your hands dirty today, brainstorm with your group five to seven acts of service that would reflect your love for God in a "physical and present" sort of way. Jot down your collective thoughts on the lines below, and then select one that you will accomplish as a group between now and when you meet again. An example has been provided to get you started.

Service Ideas

- *Ex.: Donate food to local food bank.*

- _____

- _____

- _____

- _____

- _____

- _____

- _____

❯ Close with Prayer

The end of this time together is really the beginning of enormous Good Samaritan possibility for you and your group. Take a moment to offer a prayer of thanksgiving and commitment to God, such as the one that follows.

> *Dear heavenly Father, as a group of people who love you and want to be found in faithful obedience to what you've called us to do, we ask …*
>
> *What do you want us to learn while we're on this journey toward becoming Good Samaritans?*
>
> *What is **ours** to do, as it relates to helping a world in need?*
>
> *Where would you have us start?*

start⟩ Personal Reflection

Living out your faith in real and tangible ways is more than just a six-week curriculum — it is a lifelong journey. The "Personal Reflection" section is your "diary" and "guide" as you go forward on this quest. Of course, like any journey, this one will be easier and more fruitful with the support and encouragement of others. **JustStart.org** *is that community. There you'll find other stories and testimonies just like yours, links to organizations and people who need your help and special skills, and opportunities to Learn, Live, and Lead a Good Samaritan lifestyle.*

To reconnect with this session's topic as you dive into the three-part "On Your Own" section, answer the questions below, which reference the DVD material you viewed during your small group time.

1   **2**   **3**

1. **John Ortberg** reminded you in this session's introduction that "the adventure of compassion is the journey for which you were made." What does the phrase "adventure of compassion" mean to you? Do you believe you're part of that adventure today? Note your responses in the space below.

2. Former professional football player **Miles McPherson** acknowledged that the adventure of compassion can be fantastic, but it can also be frightening. "Walking into the unknown and the unfamiliar is scary," he said, "but we have to remember that Jesus is always with us and has already paved the way for us." How does Jesus Christ convey his presence in your life? How do you know that he is near?

3. **Jim Wallis** stated, "Things change when a new generation decides, 'this that was acceptable is no longer tolerable,' or, 'that which we thought impossible, now we believe can be done.'" On the lines below, note three things that you believe must be *no longer tolerable* in this world, things that with God's power and presence you hope to see overcome.

_____

_____

_____

> **On Your Own**|START LEARNING

Everyone must **start>** *at the beginning, which means going from little or no knowledge to enough understanding to be able to make informed decisions. In each session, this portion of the Personal Reflection will provide you with resources and links to a wealth of pertinent information.*

During your group time this week, you heard Lynne Hybels tell the story of being at a conference to plan her church's AIDS ministry and hearing a Ugandan woman say, "It's great that you are working so hard to think clearly and to move forward wisely and to make all these plans, but all the time your people are planning, our people are dying."

Considering the three "no longer tolerable" things you noted on page 21, how would you rate your personal sense of urgency for seeing them come to fruition? Note your response on the continuum below.

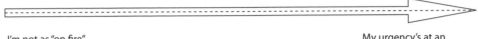

I'm not as "on fire"
as I'd like to be

My urgency's at an
all-time high!

Take a look at the "Learn" action items below. Select the one that will help heighten your sense of urgency for moving from creed to deed today!

LEARN　　　　　●○○

● **Soak in Scripture.** Meditate on Isaiah 6:8. Ask God what he would have you do to become more "sendable" today.

● **Inspire generosity.** Visit Lynne Hybels' website and read her article titled, "A Call for Unprecedented Generosity" (lynnehybels.com/articles). Make a list of ways that your family could "spend less on its wants so that [you] can give more to others' needs."

● **Take stock.** Keep track of every dollar and every hour that you invest today. Before going to bed, review your choices and ask yourself if your life is being spent in ways that honor God and those in need around you.

● **Pray dangerously.** Tell God that, like Isaiah, you are ready to "be sent" to a broken and needy world.

> **On Your Own** | START LIVING IT OUT

It is often said about salvation that it becomes real when it moves from "the head to the heart." In each session, this portion of the Personal Reflection will help you put your new knowledge into practical action and make being a Good Samaritan a part of your everyday life.

In Amos 5:21 – 24 the prophet delivers a stern warning straight from the heart of God: "I can't stand your religious meetings," it begins. "I'm fed up with your conferences and conventions. I want nothing to do with your religion projects, your pretentious slogans and goals. I'm sick of your fund-raising schemes, your public relations and image making. I've had all I can take of your noisy ego-music. When was the last time you sang to me? Do you know what I want? I want justice — oceans of it. I want fairness — rivers of it. That's what I want. That's all I want" (MSG).

Based on this passage, what does God desire that his followers find "important"? Complete the phrases below.

Oceans of _____, and rivers of _____.

In a given week, what other things vie for top spot on your list of pressing priorities? Jot down your thoughts on the lines below.

_____   _____

_____   _____

_____   _____

What attitudes or habits would need to shift in your life in order for the goals of seeking justice and pursuing fairness to top your priority list?

How might making such shifts draw you closer to the heart of God?

CHECKING IN

What "act of service" (such as helping to stock a local food bank) did you and your group select during the "Now Is the Time" portion of your time together? (See page 18.) Have you made progress in accomplishing it?

If not, seize the day!

And if you've already begun that act of service, consider taking a further step "from creed to deed" by selecting an action item from the "Live It Out" list below. Note which one would be most helpful to your spiritual growth and development in the days to come, and then ask God for the wisdom and strength to see it through.

LIVE IT OUT   ○●○

● **Talk it up.** Memorize and share Amos 5:24 with a friend or family member today. Discuss what you both believe the verse is saying.

● **Go on a need hunt.** Stop by your local shelter, fire station, nursing home, or hospital, and ask what current needs exist. Resolve to meet one simple need you uncover.

● **Invite a friend.** Ask a friend to join you at your next **start>** small group meeting. It's not too late to involve others in the quest to become Good Samaritans!

● **Give it away.** Give away a material possession to someone who needs it more than you do. Journal how it felt to put into practice the words of Acts 20:35, which says, "It is more blessed to give than to receive." (The Journal section starts on page 149.)

> **On Your Own**|START LEADING

Discipling others is often a long and difficult road, but one that brings great joy and blessing. In each session, this final portion of the Personal Reflection will help you inform and engage others in ways that will inspire and change lives.

Mother Teresa once said, "We ourselves feel that what we are doing is just a drop in the ocean. But if that drop was not in the ocean, I think the ocean would be less because of that missing drop." Based on these words, answer the following four questions in the space provided.

What do you believe you have to offer this world?

What brings you the greatest joy?

What is it that you just *can't stand* to see take place in the world?

What might God be trying to convey to you about where he wants you to "start" becoming a Good Samaritan?

Consider the following "Lead" action items, selecting and then acting on the one that will put to work your skill, your talent, and your passion.

LEAD ○○●

● **Pray to have impact; pray to be impacted.** Pray for the people whom you will meet and serve throughout this **start>** experience. Ask God not only how you might impact their lives, but also what you might learn from *them*. Lead your group in prayer along these lines the next time you meet.

● **Lead your leaders.** Encourage your church leaders to make *start> Becoming a Good Samaritan* available to the entire congregation if they haven't already done so.

● **Surf the Web.** Rally two or three small group members to join you online at just-start.org. Review the full list of contributors, praying for God to bless each one of them for their selfless contribution to **start>**.

World Vision International President Dean Hirsch says that despite the size of the issues facing the world today, whenever he has chosen to reach out and serve someone in need, even in a seemingly insignificant way, he remembers the words of Mother Teresa: "Remember, God did not call you to be successful; he called you to be faithful."

start> Ready For More?

> Read

- *The Me I Want to Be: Becoming God's Best Version of You*, John Ortberg (Zondervan)

- *Nice Girls Don't Change the World*, Lynne Hybels (Zondervan)

- *The Hole in Our Gospel*, Rich Stearns (Thomas Nelson)

- *The Irresistible Revolution: Living as an Ordinary Radical*, Shane Claiborne (Zondervan)

- *Choose Love Not Power: How to Right the World's Wrongs from a Place of Weakness*, Tony Campolo (Regal)

- *What's So Amazing About Grace?*, Philip Yancey (Zondervan)

- *Guerrilla Lovers: Changing the World with Revolutionary Compassion*, Vince Antonucci (Baker)

- *Do Something! Make Your Life Count*, Miles McPherson (Baker)

> Surf

- juststart.org

- worldvision.org

- one.org

- thecommon.org

- putyourfaithinaction.org

- passiontoaction.org

- youthworks.com

Caring for the Sick

How to fight Global Epidemics & Prevent Diseases

2

> "Let no one ever come to you without leaving better."[1] — Mother Teresa

start> Group Interaction

> Get Connected   1 minute

Have someone in the group read aloud this brief description of the session theme.

General Colin Powell said, "No war on the face of the earth is more destructive than the AIDS pandemic."[2] And with current stats on HIV/AIDS — the first epidemic of a new disease since the fifteenth century — you'd think Powell would be correct. AIDS now has spread to every country in the world; every day, nearly 7,400 people become infected with HIV and more than 5,400 people die from AIDS; and the estimated number of deaths per year is nearly two million souls.[3]

But for all of the carnage caused by AIDS, it is hardly in a category by itself. In fact, based on current United Nations findings, more children die today of malaria than of AIDS — a sobering reality, given that malaria is a preventable disease.

During this session you will be invited to take a closer look at the impact both in the U.S. and in countries abroad of pandemics such as AIDS and malaria and answer the question, "What is a Christ-follower's role in preventing and treating these fatal diseases?"

Your actions matter. Your choices matter. Choose today to **start>**.

"He heals the brokenhearted and binds up their wounds."

—Psalm 147:3

> Know Your Neighbor   2 minutes

Using one or two words, share your current beliefs or assumptions about the session theme.

> In Jesus' day, lepers were not to be touched. Who are the "untouchables" of today's society?

> Give Your Heart and Mind to God   1 minute

Followers of Jesus Christ understand that they were once "untouchable" because of their sin. But it was in the midst of that untouchable state that the God of heaven and earth wrapped himself in human flesh and came to touch the world with freedom and healing and grace. For those who have been freed, it's time to free others. For those who have been healed, it's time to heal others. For those who have tasted grace, it's time to bestow that gift on those who crave to be touched.

As you begin session 2, ask God to remind you of what it was like to be stuck in your sickness — and then to be the recipient of a healing hand to help you up. Invite him to stir you and move you and prompt you to action on behalf of someone who's sick today — whether spiritually, emotionally, financially, or physically. Ask God how you might be his conduit of healing today.

> Learn Together   30 minutes

If you'd like to take a few notes as you watch the session 2 video segment, use the space below.

> Discuss "Caring for the Sick"   20 minutes

You may not have time to discuss all of the questions in this section — that's okay! Cover as many as you can, thoughtfully, thoroughly, and with great attentiveness.

1. Think about the last time you were sick. Consider whether you had the necessary resources to find a remedy and recuperate, including things like easy access to health care, inexpensive medications, the unwavering support of family and friends, and so forth. On the grid on page 31, list the resources you had at your disposal that helped pave the path back to good health. Then, note the implications of having access to each resource, and discuss your observations with your group. An example has been provided to get you started.

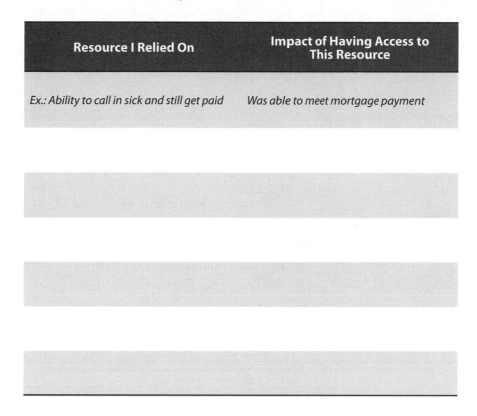

Resource I Relied On	Impact of Having Access to This Resource
Ex.: Ability to call in sick and still get paid	*Was able to meet mortgage payment*

2. For many people, poverty and disease go hand-in-hand. Take a look at the following four choices that are made week in and week out by countless thousands of people living on less than a dollar a day, and then answer the questions that follow.

Purchase malaria medication **or** Use that money to send children to school

Buy one can of clean water **or** Buy food for a week's worth of once-a-day meals

Spend money on a bed net **or** Hold the money back for a bag of grain

Inoculate newborn daughter **or** Save the money to visit dying father two countries away

Now imagine what life would be like if you had to make no-win decisions such as these on a daily or weekly basis. What are some of the spiritual, financial, emotional, physical, vocational, and relational implications you might face? Discuss your insights with your group.

3. In her teaching segment, Kay Warren linked the concepts of *pandemic disease* and *faith*. In your view, what does "faith" have to do with eradicating pandemic disease, especially when a family faces the "impossible choices" noted earlier? Jot down your thoughts in the space below before discussing them with your group.

> Now Is the Time   5 minutes

This is the most important part of the session — how your small group will put faith into action. Make each other accountable for starting today!

In this session's introduction, host John Ortberg said that while others may look past an "untouchable" person, "We can notice. We can see. We can talk. We can pray. We can help. See the sign. Hear God. *Please* touch." Think of someone you know who is sick in his or her body or who has been cast aside by "better functioning" members of society. Maybe it's a personal friend, or perhaps it is one who suffers half a world away.

How might God be asking you to reach out to that person with a loving touch from him? Write that person's name on the line at the top of the next page and then respond to the four starter ideas below it.

God, help me to touch: _____

The needs that I see in his/her life:

What I can say:

What I can pray:

How I can help:

> Close with Prayer   1 minute

The end of this time together is really the beginning of enormous Good Samaritan possibility for you and your group. Take a moment to offer a prayer of thanksgiving and commitment to God, such as the one that follows.

> *We pray that you lay your hands on our brothers and sisters of Africa [and around the world]: the mothers, fathers, daughters, and sons. We pray that you touch their lives with your presence, your love, and your grace. We pray that you heal their hearts and minds with the gift of life. We pray that you heal the church. We pray that you touch the hearts, minds, and souls of all religious communities with your compelling hand of truth. We pray that you heal our fear, our anxiety, and our prejudice that we might live lives of faith, hope, and love to touch those suffering from [diseases such as] HIV/AIDS.*
>
> *— From A Prayer for Africa, the aWAKE Project [4]*

start⟩ Personal Reflection

Living out your faith in real and tangible ways is more than just a six-week curriculum — it is a lifelong journey. The "Personal Reflection" section is your "diary" and "guide" as you go forward on this quest. Of course, like any journey, this one will be easier and more fruitful with the support and encouragement of others. **JustStart.org** *is that community. There you'll find other stories and testimonies just like yours, links to organizations and people who need your help and special skills, and opportunities to Learn, Live, and Lead a Good Samaritan lifestyle.*

To reconnect with this session's topic as you dive into the three-part "On Your Own" section, answer the questions below, which reference the DVD material you viewed during your small group time.

1. Session teacher **Kay Warren** said that after her first trip to Africa, she found herself judging not other people, but herself. "I had to ask, What would I do? What *was* I doing?" Kay said. "And the answer was, *nothing.*" When have you ever found yourself in a similar situation, feeling fearful and overwhelmed as you consider the AIDS pandemic? Note the fears or emotions you felt in the space below.

The Fatal Four

Cholera

Agent: bacterium [Vibrio cholera]
First recorded: 1563
Region: Africa, Asia, and Latin America
Symptoms: falling temperature and blood pressure; vomiting/rapid dehydration; organ failure; stomach cramps; severe diarrhea; leg cramps
Treatment: [clean] fluids and salt intake, or "oral rehydration therapy"; some antibiotics; some vaccines

HIV and AIDS

Agent: virus [Human Immunodeficiency Virus]
First recorded: 1959
Region: global
Symptoms: weakened immune system leading to infection with other diseases, especially tuberculosis
Treatment: ARV cocktail, or "highly active antiretroviral therapy" including three or more drugs ingested at a time

Malaria

Agent: protozoan and mosquito [Plasmodium falciparum, Plasmodium vivax, Plasmodium ovale, and Plasmodium malariae]
First recorded: antiquity
Region: tropics and subtropics
Symptoms: fever; chills; headache; fatigue; possible vomiting; possible nausea; possible diarrhea
Treatment: so far, no vaccine has been developed, and parasites are good at becoming resistant to drugs; prevention is proving the greatest weapon and centers on insecticide-treated bed nets

Tuberculosis (TB)

Agent: bacterium [Mycobacterium tuberculosis complex]
First recorded: antiquity
Region: global
Symptoms: fever; fatigue; possible facial scarring; coughing; deterioration of lungs; chest pain; appetite loss; weight loss; possible stomach, bladder, and kidney problems; general muscle wastage
Treatment: combination of antibiotics for at least a six-month period[5]

2. In this session's wrap, host **John Ortberg** said, "There's a Ugandan saying to the effect that one plus one becomes a bundle. One compassionate heart. One act of mercy. One trip to see people in need. One generous check. One person, and then one more, and then one more, and then it starts to form a bundle of compassion and kindness and good that can make a significant difference in a world of darkness and suffering like our own." When have you been helped toward healing by the kindness or generosity of "just one person"?

3. Global AIDS expert **Christo Greyling** said that upon manifesting his first AIDS symptoms, he knew that time was running out. Greyling told his wife, "I want to be a witness for Christ, using this situation of HIV while I'm still healthy enough to do it." As you consider your own life, what are you "healthy enough to do" today in terms of helping eradicate preventable disease? Before you move into this session's "On Your Own" sections, complete the following sentences:

In doing my part to help eradicate preventable or treatable disease, I could _____, which might lead to _____, which might lead to _____ or even _____.

I could also envision myself _____, which God might use to _____. Truth be told, I'm even healthy enough to _____, which might mean _____ for all sorts of people in need of God's healing touch!

might mean _____for all sorts of people in need of God's healing touch!

Now you can see for yourself what it's like to live with AIDS. "World Vision Experience: AIDS" offers an online look at the lives of two children — Olivia and Stephen — living in AIDS-affected communities in Africa. The experience takes only a few minutes but has the power to change your perspective for the rest of your life. Visit media.worldvision.org/getinvolved/ aids_experience/index.html to begin your journey of understanding today.

> **On Your Own**|START LEARNING

In Exodus 15:26, God made a covenant of healing with his people and said that if they would keep all of his commandments, he would be their health and healer continually. Literally, he was naming himself *Jehovah Rapha* — the "God who heals."

If God *always* holds power to heal, what might be his purposes for sometimes choosing not to heal in the way we would like? Note your responses in the space below.

Likewise, if God is the only one who ultimately possesses the power to heal, what do you suppose the role of Christ-followers should be in helping to eradicate diseases like AIDS and malaria?

Review the "Learn" action items that follow, noting the one(s) that God might be prompting you to pursue now.

LEARN ●○○

● **Give thanks for good health.** Flip to the Journal section of this guide, which begins on page 149, and respond to Dr. Thomas Fuller's eighteenth-century quote, "Health is not valued till sickness comes."[6] What thoughts, values, or beliefs do his words stir up in your spirit?

● **Visit your own backyard.** Is there someone in your community who is actively involved in meeting the needs of people suffering with preventable and treatable diseases? Invite them to participate in your **start>** discussions to glean insights and learn of user-friendly ways you and your group might participate locally.

● **Watch your water.** The EPA estimates that more than 80 percent of infant mortality in the undeveloped world is attributable to unsafe drinking water. Assuming you have access to clean drinking water, as a way to get in touch with just how fortunate you are, log your water intake for one full day. Each time you brush your teeth, take a shower, or down a quick eight ounces of cool refreshment, offer a prayer of thanksgiving to God.

● **Pray for healing.** Get out your calendar and highlight days that celebrate various countries or the holidays of various faith traditions. Pray for the people of that country who are being affected by global health issues and then participate in a service project that reflects your compassion. For example, you might celebrate Chinese New Year by collaborating on a community service project with a local Chinese church congregation. On World AIDS Day — December 1 — you could invite people to make a donation toward the eradication of this disease. Visit earthcalendar.net for a complete listing of holidays by date, country, and religion.

"When the history books are written, our age will be remembered for three things: the war on terror, the digital revolution, and what we did—or did not do–to put out the fire in Africa."[7]

— Bono

> **On Your Own**|START LIVING IT OUT

Read Matthew 10:1 – 9 below, paying close attention to the *message* Jesus asks his followers to preach, the *mission* he asks them to accomplish, and the *motivation* that is to characterize their work. Then complete the sentences and answer the questions that follow.

> *Jesus called his twelve disciples to him and gave them authority to drive out evil spirits and to heal every disease and sickness. These are the names of the twelve apostles: first, Simon (who is called Peter) and his brother Andrew; James son of Zebedee, and his brother John; Philip and Bartholomew; Thomas and Matthew the tax collector; James son of Alphaeus, and Thaddaeus; Simon the Zealot and Judas Iscariot, who betrayed him.*
>
> *These twelve Jesus sent out with the following instructions: "Do not go among the Gentiles or enter any town of the Samaritans. Go rather to the lost sheep of Israel. As you go, proclaim this message: 'The kingdom of heaven has come near.' Heal the sick, raise the dead, cleanse those who have leprosy, drive out demons. Freely you have received, freely give." (emphasis added)*

Jesus sent out his early followers, asking them to tell people that

_____.

As part of their mission they were to accomplish four works, including:

healing _____,

raising _____,

cleansing _____,

and driving out _____.

The motivation that was to undergird his disciples' actions was this:

"Freely _____, freely _____."

Your ability to fulfill Christ's first-century instruction in a twenty-first century world begins with putting yourself in the shoes of someone who is in need of cleansing and healing. Imagine the life of someone who is chronically ill — a modern-day leper, if you will. On the grid below, list some of the hopes and dreams you envision them carrying each day of their lives. The dreams might be simple in nature (i.e., "to be hugged," "to have people make eye contact with me") or more complex (i.e., "to be freed from paralysis and able to walk for the first time in my life"). Let your imagination run free as you consider what it must be like to be outcast or sick in your body.

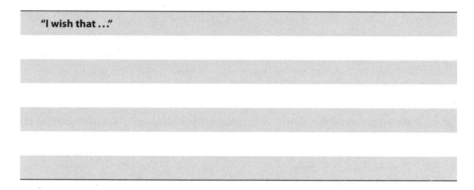

"I wish that . . ."

Jesus Christ was specific in Matthew 10 that his followers' motivation for bringing help and healing to a world in need was to be the remembrance of their own healing in him. "Freely you have received," he says, "freely give." As you consider his exhortation, note in the grid below what things you have "freely received" from Christ. An example has been provided.

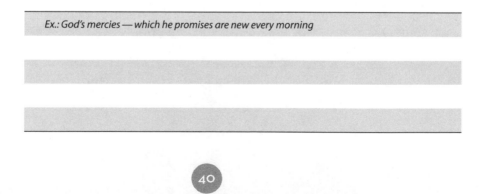

Ex.: God's mercies — which he promises are new every morning

Have you ever thought about the fact that God has freely given you specific resources so that you might turn toward others and freely share those resources with them? After taking a look at your completed grid, note in the space below how you might use one of the resources you already possess to provide help and healing to someone in need today.

CHECKING IN

During the "Now Is the Time" portion of your small group time for this session (see pages 32–33), you noted the name of one person in your life whom you might reach out and "touch" in a meaningful way. How has God honored your openness to meeting a practical need in that person's life? Record your thoughts below, then consider another step of service from the "Live It Out" list on page 42.

LIVE IT OUT

● **Lend your voice.** Lend your voice to people suffering with HIV and AIDS by joining the ONE Campaign today. Visit one.org for details.

● **Love a child.** Sponsor a HopeChild through World Vision and help turn the tide on AIDS by responding to the specific needs of children in communities affected by the disease. Your monthly gift provides a child and his or her community with access to critical basics such as improved nutrition, health care, clean water, school fees and supplies, and vocational training, plus age-appropriate, values-based HIV-prevention education, counseling, support for local care networks, and trained local volunteers to look after the needs of vulnerable children and help care for sick or dying parents. For details visit worldvision.org/start.

● **Take an "H₂O Challenge."** Assuming you have no health restrictions, for two weeks drink nothing but water and donate the money you would normally spend on coffee, soda, smoothies, and other beverages to World Vision or another organization that drills clean-water wells in developing countries. Journal your observations as you go through the two-week experiment in the Journal section that begins on page 149.

● **Act on AIDS.** Join the *Acting on AIDS* grassroots movement to raise awareness, promote advocacy, and be transformed in response to global AIDS and related issues of injustice. Individual students as well as campus organizations and ministries take part in creative activism and discipleship efforts to transform hearts on campuses as well as turn the tide of global AIDS. For more information, visit worldvision.org/start.

● **Purchase a net; save a life.** In the fall of 2008, the United Nations announced $3.2 billion in new funding to cover all 600 million people at risk of malaria with bed nets and medication by December 31, 2010.[8] For ten dollars, you can be part of helping reach that goal. Visit endmalaria.org for details.

● **Teach the truth.** According to "Unite for Children, Unite against AIDS," one of the most important ways to serve those with HIV/AIDS is to alert people in your local church, school, community, and workplace to the fact that HIV/AIDS is a disease that affects *millions* of children. Dispel the myth that HIV/AIDS is an adults-only disease by hosting or agreeing to speak at your next PTA meeting, Sunday school class, or workplace staff meeting. Visit World Vision online at worldvisionresources. com to gather helpful teaching resources.

● **Give care.** Assemble a Caregiver Kit that equips a trained World Vision frontline caregiver with essential supplies such as soap, washcloths, and latex gloves that can improve and prolong the lives of those living with AIDS, as well as help prevent the spread of the disease. For more information, go to worldvision.org/start.

> **On Your Own**|START LEADING

Sandy Thurman, former director of the Office of National AIDS Policy, said, "When someone shares that they are HIV-positive, the first thing that comes to our minds should *not* be, 'What did you do?' but rather, 'What can *I* do?'"

What thoughts or feelings are elicited by Thurman's assertion? Write them down in the space below.

Which aspects of Christ's character are on display when you ask not, "What did you do?" but instead, "What can *I* do for you?" Three examples have been provided. Add your own ideas to the mix.

Ex.: availability, selflessness, service

Select one item from those noted above that you'd like to work on between now and session 3. Then, choose a "Lead" item from the list on page 44 that can help you to practice that character trait.

LEAD ○○●

● **Invite God's intervention.** Facilitate a weekly or monthly prayer group that meets for a defined period of time and focuses on understanding and interceding for global health issues. Consider highlighting one people group, country, or disease each time you convene, and then invite participants to serve in ways that stretch them emotionally, spiritually, and financially between sessions. Visit worldvision.org for country-by-country analysis and insight.

● **Grab a pen and paper.** Write to challenge your local, national, and international leaders not only to recognize the effect of HIV and AIDS on children but to make sure that children have a prominent place in the discussions about eradicating this terrible disease. Google "representative contact information" for your particular state, city, or community to gather the necessary addresses.

● **Get cooking!** Coordinate an event, such as a breakfast gathering or a dinner fundraiser, with an area college or university to raise awareness and energize students about getting involved in the fight against preventable or treatable diseases. Be sure to provide suggestions for straightforward ways that students and staff can make a quick-hitting, tangible difference in their corner of the world, such as by hosting town hall meetings, sponsoring fun-runs to raise money for the cause, hosting book clubs, and so forth. Departments that would most likely collaborate include humanities, social sciences, religious studies, or the school of social work.

● **Discover what's working well.** Locally, partner with organizations that are already engaging in global issues and invite groups of people to attend the events and participate in the discussion forums. Local chapters of the United Nations Association of the USA are a good place to start and can be found by visiting unusa.org. For global health discussion ideas, visit who.org or reliefweb.net.

● **Host a guest speaker.** Invite a guest speaker to your Sunday school class, ministry team meeting, or **start>** small group to help educate your community on effective ways to serve sufferers of pandemics worldwide.

● **Find your match.** Obtain corporate financial "matches" to your individual relief efforts by developing rapport with the community service coordinator in your workplace or at the companies where friends and family members work. (If the role doesn't exist in your organization, consider creating and then filling it!)

● **Take flight.** Organize an educational/missional trip to an African nation, where the firsthand effects of pandemics like AIDS and malaria are prevalent. Partner with a ministry or non-governmental organization (NGO) so that your group will be prepared for particular areas of service and educational experiences. During the weeks leading up to the trip, develop team unity and trust; pray together; raise your awareness about the country, culture, and most pressing issues; discuss anxieties and expectations; and participate in film or book discussions that highlight global disease and the country you plan to visit. Then debrief toward the end of the trip and again after you return home. As a group, implement at least one aspect of your experience within the context of your continued hometown efforts.

Ready for More?

> Read

- *Say Yes to God: A Call to Courageous Surrender*, Kay Warren (Zondervan)

- *Warrior Princess: Fighting for Life with Courage and Hope*, Princess Kasune Zulu (IVP)

- *A Positive Life: Living with HIV as a Pastor, Husband, and Father*, Shane Stanford (Zondervan)

- *Love Mercy*, Lisa Samson and Ty Samson (Zondervan)

- *The AIDS Crisis: What We Can Do*, Deborah Dortzbach and W. Meredith Long (IVP)

- *HIV/AIDS: A Very Short Introduction*, Alan Whiteside (Oxford University Press)

- *The Son of God Is Dancing: A Message of Hope*, Adrian and Bridget Plass (Authentic Media)

- *Blue Covenant: The Global Water Crisis and the Coming Battle for the Right to Water*, Maude Barlow (New Press)

- *The Fever: How Malaria Has Ruled Humankind for 500,000 Years*, Sonia Shah (Farrar, Straus and Giroux)

- *Water: The Fate of Our Most Precious Resource*, Marq de Villiers (Mariner)

- *A Guide to Acting on AIDS*, World Vision Resources

- *Water Wars: Privatization, Pollution, and Profit*, Vandana Shiva (South End Press)

> Watch

- *Beyond Borders* Internet Television

- *Medicines for Malaria* Venture (mmv.org)

- *Wash: Life without Water* (youtube.com)

> Surf

- juststart.org

- worldvision.org

- one.org

- thepeaceplan.com

- charitywater.org

- endmalaria.org

- globalhealth.org

- bloodwatermission.com

Seeking Justice and Reconciliation

How fairness Changes People, Communities, & Nations

3

> "God has a plan to help bring justice to the world — and his plan is us!"
>
> — Gary Haugen, founder of International Justice Mission

start> Group Interaction

> Get Connected   1 minute

Have someone in the group read aloud this brief description of the session theme.

All people are "God's kind" of people — people who were created in the image of Almighty God and for an intentional purpose. And while most Christ-followers agree that all people should be treated with dignity and respect, their spheres of influence can become strangely homogenous, filled only with friends who look, act, talk, dress, and vote just like them. It's a far cry from what Jesus Christ intended when he instructed his followers to serve as light and salt in a dark, bland world.

What is the Christian's role in reconciling broken and bruised relationships in today's world? It is, according to the well-known words of Micah 6:8, to "do justice, and to love kindness, and to walk humbly with your God" (RSV). It's an interesting triad to consider because it implies that kindness and humility alone are not enough. It is the seeking out of *justice*, as well, that will prove to a watching world that the God we serve is good.

Your actions matter. Your choices matter. Choose today to **start>**.

"To do what is right and just is more acceptable to the LORD than sacrifice."

—Proverbs 21:3

> Know Your Neighbor   2 minutes

Using one or two words, share your current beliefs or assumptions about the session theme.

Where does "injustice" exist in today's world?

> Give Your Heart and Mind to God   1 minute

In Isaiah 1:16–17, the prophet conveyed instruction on God's behalf according to a vision he had regarding Judah and Jerusalem. "Cease to do evil," said Isaiah, "learn to do good; seek justice, correct oppression; bring justice to the fatherless, plead the widow's cause" (RSV).

It's clear that God has high expectations for his followers' involvement in eradicating injustices in the world in which they live, but equally important is God's expectation for what they will do *before* they seek justice. In the verse that precedes Isaiah's litany of commands, he tells the people — and Christ-followers today — to "wash yourselves; make yourselves clean; remove the evil of your deeds from before my eyes."

As you enter into session 3, ask God to show you areas in your life that need to be washed clean by his supernatural power, so that you will be able to approach the task of justice-seeking with pure hands and a spotless heart.

> Learn Together   30 minutes

If you'd like to take a few notes as you watch the session 3 video segment, use the space below.

> Discuss "Seeking Justice and Reconciliation"   20 minutes

You may not have time to discuss all of the questions in this section — that's okay! Cover as many as you can, thoughtfully, thoroughly, and with great attentiveness.

1. Gary Haugen, founder of International Justice Mission, defined injustice as taking from people what's inherently theirs. Among your small group, what "common inheritances" do you enjoy? Note your answers on the grid below, and then discuss your insights. An example has been provided to get you started.

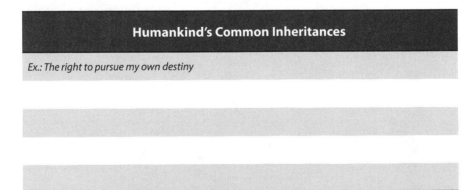

Humankind's Common Inheritances
Ex.: The right to pursue my own destiny

2. "God wants to do his work of justice in the world," said Haugen, "but he invites us to be his plan — his instruments — for doing it." Who comes to mind when you think of someone who has invested his or her life to make sure other people could realize their common inheritance? What did their involvement look like?

3. David Anderson, author and founding pastor of Bridgeway Community Church in Columbia, Maryland, calls people who get involved in making sure everyone enjoys the protections of justice and "positive favor" — regardless of their color, class, or culture — "gracists." Gracism, then, is a shorthand way of referring to God's desire for all of his followers, that those who claim his name would love *everyone* well. With that goal in mind, discuss the three truths about gracists that follow.

Truth #1: Gracists recognize their own need for grace.

When have you been in a situation in which you craved grace or inclusion from another person — perhaps a parent, a friend, or a boss? Talk about your experience with your group, considering the following questions:

- Did you receive the inclusion you sought?

- How does "being included" heighten your willingness to extend grace and inclusion to others?

Truth #2: Gracists include, not exclude, others.

Think about your closest friends, family members, colleagues, and trusted confidants. To borrow a phrase from David Anderson, these people make up your "circle of honor." In the circle below, write the names of several people who are in your circle of honor.

Now take a look at the names you listed in your circle of honor. Are there common denominators that you notice regarding color, class, or culture? Summarize your sampling by completing the sentences below, and then share your findings with your group.

The most common skin color represented in my sampling is_____

_____.

The most common economic class represented is_____

_____.

The most common culture or heritage represented is_____

_____.

Now consider who is *missing* from the circle. Discuss your answers to the following three questions with your group:

- When you consider honestly who might be missing from your circle, what *color* are they?

- What socioeconomic *class* are they from?

- What *culture(s)* do they represent?

The way your circle of honor is currently comprised might be a function of how you were raised. Take a look at the messages in the box below, some of which may have been instilled in you or your friends, and then discuss your reactions with the other members of your group.

"There's *us*, and then there are *those people*."

"Hold your purse tight when someone from *that* group walks by."

"Lock the doors to your house if you ever see *them* drive by."

"Rich people are greedy."

"Poor people are lazy."

"*Those* people are just white trash."

"They're idiots. Just ignore them."

"Boys should be president, and girls should be pregnant."

"You're not friends unless you worship at the same church."

"Fat people are slobs."

"Nobody would do that job but a _____."

"Don't go near *them* ... they're dirty."

"Keep your distance. He's a creepy old man."

What messages, assumptions, or circumstances may have influenced the composition of *your* circle of honor? Record your insights on the lines below before sharing your thoughts with your group.

_____

_____

_____

_____

Truth #3: Gracists foster and relish diversity in the kingdom of God.

Part of becoming a gracist is respecting all men, women, and children as creations of God. Soong-Chan Rah, professor at North Park Seminary in Chicago, conducted a research study that features the following findings:

1950	2008
The "typical" Christian was an upper middle class, white male who resided in suburbia.	The "typical" Christian was a Nigerian peasant, a university student in Seoul, or a Latin American teenager.
Christians were 80 percent white, predominantly from western countries, and residents of the northern hemisphere.	The demographic makeup of Christians was 40 percent white with the majority residing in the southern hemisphere and eastern nations.
The center of Christianity is no longer the United States or Western Europe, but Africa, Asia, and Latin America.	Thirty-three percent of Christians were in the minority population, and it is projected that by 2050, 80 percent of Christians will be non-white.

How do your perceptions of "typical" Christians stack up to the statistics noted on page 54? Discuss your thoughts with your group.

> Now Is the Time   5 minutes

This is the most important part of the session — how your small group will put faith into action. Make each other accountable for starting today!

Brenda Salter McNeil mentioned that part of her bridge-building efforts toward relating with Latin immigrants includes her taking Spanish language lessons. What actions — whether small or large — might help you begin to build bridges toward inclusion of *all* of God's people, regardless of their color, their class, or their culture? Jot down your ideas in the space below, and then share one or two of them with your group. Then, select one item from your list to pursue between now and the next time your group convenes. Two examples have been provided to get you started.

Bridge-Building Actions I Can Take
Ex.: Take Spanish language lessons.
Ex.: Be the first person in a social situation this week to extend a hand of friendship to someone who seems the most "unlike" me.

❯ Close with Prayer

The end of this time together is really the beginning of enormous Good Samaritan possibility for you and your group. Take a moment to offer a prayer of thanksgiving and commitment to God, such as the one that follows.

> *Father, we call Thee Father because we love Thee. We are glad to be called Thy children, and to dedicate our lives to the service that extends through willing hearts and hands to the betterment of all mankind. We send a cry of Thanksgiving for people of all races, creeds, classes, and colors the world over, and pray that through the instrumentality of our lives the spirit of peace, joy, fellowship, and brotherhood shall circle the world. We know that this world is filled with discordant notes, but help us, Father, to so unite our efforts that we may all join in one harmonious symphony for peace and brotherhood, justice, and equality of opportunity for all men. The tasks performed today with forgiveness for all our errors, we dedicate, dear Lord, to Thee. Grant us strength and courage and faith and humility sufficient for the tasks assigned to us.*

— Mary McLeod Bethune,
daughter of slaves; sister of sixteen
siblings; columnist; educator; prayer
warrior; and indefatigable voice for
global equality before, during, and
after World War II

start *Personal Reflection*

Living out your faith in real and tangible ways is more than just a six-week curriculum — it is a lifelong journey. The "Personal Reflection" section is your "diary" and "guide" as you go forward on this quest. Of course, like any journey, this one will be easier and more fruitful with the support and encouragement of others. **JustStart.org** *is that community. There you'll find other stories and testimonies just like yours, links to organizations and people who need your help and special skills, and opportunities to Learn, Live, and Lead a Good Samaritan lifestyle.*

To reconnect with this session's topic as you dive into the three-part "On Your Own" section, answer the questions below, which reference the DVD material you viewed during your small group time.

1   2   3

1. **Gary Haugen** said that two of the more unfamiliar passions of God are his passion for *the world* and his passion for *justice*. If your family and close friends were polled, how well would they say your life reflects these two passions? Are you satisfied with what you assume they would say? Why or why not?

2. **Brenda Salter McNeil** said that while it is normal to want to stay in our comfort zones, "if we are going to win back the credibility of the church, it's going to take us smack dab through 'Samaria,'" the place where you might feel uncomfortable, unknown, and unloved.

How might your willingness to venture into "Samaria" help you to embrace a passion for the world and a passion for justice *equally*, as does God?

3. Teen activist **Zach Hunter** began his work toward abolishing slavery when he was a preteen. "There's a place at the table of activism even for a twelve-year-old!" he said. Hunter didn't allow his youthfulness to keep him from getting in the game. What are a few of the perceived obstacles you see in *your* life that threaten to keep you sidelined from making a difference in the areas of justice and racial reconciliation? Note them in the space below; then, ask God to help replace your fears and assumptions with confidence and strength as you work through the "On Your Own" questions in the coming days.

> **On Your Own**|START LEARNING

Lydia Bean, a board member for Friends of Justice, a faith-based organization that defends due process in the criminal justice system, recently wrote an article for *Sojourners* magazine titled, "Bridging the Great Divide," which explores what it looks like to proclaim the gospel and invite people to follow Jesus in a way that leads to the work of justice. After reading her comments, respond to the questions that follow.

A friend recently attended a liberal church where the pastor constantly talked about the "gospel of inclusion." My friend asked me, "Why didn't she just talk about the gospel — *why add qualifications?" I suspect it was to avoid confusion with that* other *gospel — you know, the one that those tacky fundamentalists preach.*

And so, when evangelicals and liberal Christians get together, we avoid conflict by avoiding the gospel. Oh, we talk about the gospel — *in the abstract. Both sides agree that the gospel is personal, but never private. We hammer out its policy implications. But we never proclaim "the gospel" itself. That would force us to admit that we have totally different understandings of what the "good news" is.*

Pretty soon, it falls apart. Evangelicals start wondering if all this justice work will distract them from sharing the gospel — as if these were unrelated priorities. Liberals get uncomfortable with all that talk about personal salvation — can't we just get on with political activism? According to New Testament scholar N. T. Wright, neither side has the whole gospel.

As Wright sums it up, the gospel is the good news that Jesus is Lord — Jesus, the crucified Messiah, has been raised from the dead and the new creation is coming. In his book Surprised by Hope, *Wright sets the gospel within the Bible's larger story: "God created a good creation, mourned the fall of humanity, raised up Israel to model a better way, and then sent Jesus to set the whole world right. Jesus died on the cross to carry out God's justice — his promise to set the world right and flood all creation with his glory."*[1]

According to Bean, there exists a continuum in Christendom where one end focuses solely on personal salvation and the other solely on political/social justice. Where would you say you land on such a continuum? Mark your response with an X below.

Emphasis on personal salvation   Emphasis on social justice

If N. T. Wright is correct, and the Bible places emphasis on *both* areas — personal salvation *and* social justice — then why do you think people in today's world are polarized on this subject?

As you select a "Learn" activity from the list below to focus on this week, think about how the action you take might accomplish both goals, the goal of pointing people toward faith in Jesus Christ and the goal of meeting their practical needs.

LEARN   ●○○

● **Get in the loop.** Join the Not for Sale Campaign's (notforsalecampaign.org) e-distribution list to stay aware of opportunities for joining the fight against injustice, both in the United States and around the world.

● **Shop responsibly.** The book *The Better World Shopper* (New Society Publishers, 2008; betterworldshopper.org) provides the latest information on more than one hundred of the largest U.S. companies with the most popular brands across twenty-five industries. Use their research and information to determine which companies you should avoid and which ones are moving toward economic, social, and environmental responsibility.

● **Crash with a few friends.** Rent the film *Crash* (Lions Gate Entertainment, 2004, rated "R") and view it with several friends. Afterward, have each person in the group share his or her "crash moments" and the impact they've made on life.

● **End the blame game.** Visit tenshek-elshirt.com to view the video of the song "It's Not Your Fault" by the band 10 Shekel Shirt. Consider your current understanding of issues around trafficking, drug addiction, prostitution, and racism as you view the video, and then flip to the Journal section of this guide, which begins on page 149, to record your perceptions and assumptions about whether people who suffer injustice in the world are to blame for their plight. How would you like to see these people treated by Christ's followers in days to come?

"Injustice anywhere is a threat to justice everywhere. We are caught in an inescapable network of mutuality, tied in a single garment of destiny. Whatever affects one directly, affects all indirectly." [2]

—Martin Luther King Jr.

> **On Your Own**|START LIVING IT OUT

The words of Micah 6:6 – 8 say:

> *With what shall I come before the* L*ORD* *and bow down before the exalted God? Shall I come before him with burnt offerings, with calves a year old? Will the* L*ORD* *be pleased with thousands of rams, with ten thousand rivers of oil? Shall I offer my firstborn for my transgression, the fruit of my body for the sin of my soul? He has shown all you people what is good. And what does the* L*ORD* *require of you? To act justly and to love mercy and to walk humbly with your God.*

Lovers of God are to act justly, because **God is just**.

They are to love mercy, because **God is merciful**.

They are to walk humbly with their God, because **God is holy**.

> How have you observed those three character traits of God being played out in your life? Think back on your life experience, and then complete the sentences below.
>
> I've seen God's *justice* when …
>
>
> I've seen God's *mercy* when…
>
>
> I've seen God's *holiness* when…
>
>
> Why do you suppose it is so important to God that his followers strike the balance of manifesting those same three characteristics — justice, mercy, and holiness — in their lives?

What aspect of your attitude or personality would you ask God to shift so that you could become a more fully orbed reflection of the character of God in this regard? Make your request in the form of a prayer on the lines below.

_____

_____

_____

_____

_____

_____

CHECKING IN

Think about the " Now Is the Time" commitment you made at the close of your small group time (see page 55). For Brenda Salter McNeil, her bridge-building action was Spanish language lessons. Which bridge-building action did *you* agree to take, and how are you doing in terms of progress? Note your response in the space below.

If you're ready for a more significant challenge, scan the five "Live It Out" action items on the next page and select one that you'd like to try today.

LIVE IT OUT

● **Act on what you've learned.** Join the social justice committee at your place of worship. If there isn't one, consider starting one with other community leaders. Check with missions coordinators for insight about how to establish a local outreach program in your community of faith.

● **Speak your mind!** Become an advocate for social justice by writing to your elected officials and media organizations about social justice issues that concern you the most. Visit congress.org to locate contact information and the International Justice Mission (ijm. org) for sample letters.

● **Provoke your friends.** Invite your small group or circle of friends to log onto Provoke Radio (provokeradio.com) and join you in listening to an archived discussion about faith and social justice.

● **Read … and then act.** Select a book from the list on pages 66–67 of this guide and host a book club to learn how other people have put their compassion into action to combat injustices around the globe. Commit as a group to taking a simple next step, such as joining the Not for Sale Campaign e-distribution after reading *Not for Sale*.

● **Go glocal.** Turn your group into a "glocal" community by thinking globally and acting locally. Agree to meet once a month to discuss one pressing global issue, such as the ones presented in *start> Becoming a Good Samaritan*. During your meetings, pray over the people groups being affected, and then commit to taking action to help alleviate an evident problem they face. Better still, coincide a culturally relevant meal with each group meeting!

> **On Your Own|**START LEADING

In February 2009, blogger Eugene Cho published a post titled, "10 Reasons We Don't Like to Talk about Race." As the church, "we talk often of the reconciliation that is necessary between God and humanity," Cho wrote, "but we need to keep pushing forward with how that faith informs and transforms our relationship with one another."

So, why is it that "interpersonal reconciliation" is such a difficult subject to broach? In Cho's words, there are at least ten reasons why. What follows on page 64 is an excerpt from sojo.net.

10 Reasons We Don't Like to Talk about Race

1. It's hard work. And people can be lazy. And talking about racism is an exhausting conversation because it brings up some deep questions. Reconciliation is hard work.

2. A little something called Life. There are lots of other things going on … like the financial recession.

3. Confusion. People don't like confusion. Folks like clarity and certainty. We like answers.

4. Conflict. People don't like conflict and, well, the conversation of racism provokes conflict and strong opinions.

5. Fear. People are afraid—afraid to consider the possibilities that we're racist, prejudiced, or implicated by our silence; afraid to consider that we live as victims in a "victimized" mentality; afraid to consider that we need to "give up" something; afraid to "count the costs."

6. Apathy. People don't care. We're apathetic. And this is probably the scariest reason.

7. We don't think it exists. What racism? What prejudice? And this reason is probably equally as scary as #6.

8. People don't know how to talk about racism. We don't have an agreed upon framework to engage the conversation and move toward peace and reconciliation.

9. We want to forget the past and just "move forward." It's over. Heck, Obama is president. It's a new day.

10. [Insert your own additional reasons here …]

"The topics of racism, prejudice, and reconciliation are indeed painful conversations," Cho concludes. "While I don't necessarily believe that the answer lies exclusively with the church, I do believe the answer lies with the gospel. It lies ultimately with the message of *shalom* that God intended for humanity to live in fellowship with God and with one another—each who is created in the image of God."[3]

In the top-ten list on page 64, circle the items that most resonate with you. Then, review the list of "Lead" opportunities below and select one that will help begin to overcome the obstacles *you* face on the subject of discussing and eradicating racism and injustice.

LEAD ○○●

Rally your block. Organize a get together such as a block party with your neighbors, and invite a local outreach coordinator to be the speaker. Ask him or her to explain opportunities that exist in your own backyard for fighting for others' basic human rights.

Leverage other people's work. Host a panel discussion with several leaders who are already putting their compassion into action in the fight against the sex and labor trade.

Host a justice meal. Have your church or ministry team host a simple meal (visit worldvision.org and search "Broken Bread" for ideas) and ask the participants to make a donation that will be given to a local organization that works for justice in your community (ex., a group like Lutheran Family Services that assists with refugee resettlement).

Facilitate a talking film. Organize and host a "talking film" at your home or church. Show a film such as *Sacrifice* (Bruno Films, brunofilms.com) and then facilitate a thought-provoking discussion with those in attendance. Be sure to designate your discussion facilitators ahead of time, as well as to plan a decent block of time for accomplishing both objectives — viewing of the movie and the thorough discussion afterward.

Go back to school. Seek out the educators in your community and link arms to tutor children who are struggling in local schools.

Become a Big Brother or a Big Sister. If the organization doesn't have a chapter in your town, then start one! Contact other chapters to learn the most effective ways to serve children who need godly role models in their lives. Better still, collaborate with your church's children's department in serving a larger number of boys and girls who would benefit from a program like Big Brothers/Big Sisters of America (bbbs.org).

start> Ready for More?

> Read

- *Terrify No More: Young Girls Held Captive and the Daring Undercover Operation to Win Their Freedom*, Gary A. Haugen and Gregg Hunter (Thomas Nelson)

- *Just Courage: God's Great Expedition for the Restless Christian*, Gary A. Haugen (IVP)

- *Be the Change: Your Guide to Freeing Slaves and Changing the World*, Zach Hunter (Zondervan/Youth Specialties)

- *Not for Sale: The Return to the Global Slave Trade—and How We Fight It*, David Batstone (HarperOne)

- *A Long Way Gone: Memoirs of a Boy Soldier*, Ishmael Beah (Farrar, Straus and Giroux)

- *Sex Trafficking: Inside the Business of Modern Slavery*, Siddharth Kara (Columbia University Press)

- *Escaping the Devil's Bedroom: Sex Trafficking, Global Prostitution, and the Gospel's Transforming Power*, Dawn Herzog Jewell (Monarch)

- *A Credible Witness: Reflections on Power, Evangelism and Race*, Brenda Salter McNeil (IVP)

- *Gracism: The Art of Inclusion*, David A. Anderson (IVP)

- *Rediscovering Values: On Wall Street, Main Street, and Your Street*, Jim Wallis (Howard)

- *Let Justice Roll Down*, John Perkins (Regal)

- *Ethnic Blends: Mixing Diversity into Your Local Church*, Mark DeYmaz and Harry Li (Zondervan)

- *Divided by Faith: Evangelical Religion and the Problem of Race in America*, Michael O. Emerson and Christian Smith (Oxford University Press)

- *Rabble-Rouser for Peace: The Authorized Biography of Desmond Tutu*, John Allen (Free Press)

- *A Story of Rhythm and Grace: What the Church Can Learn from Rock and Roll about Healing the Racial Divide*, Jimi Calhoun (Brazos)

> Watch

- *The Blind Side* (Alcon Entertainment, 2009, rated "PG–13")

- *The Mission* (Warner Bros. Pictures, 1986, rated "PG")

- *We Were Free* (International Justice Mission, 2008, not rated)

> Surf

- juststart.org

- ijm.org (International Justice Mission)

- notforsalecampaign.org

- saltermcneil.com

- mosaix.info

- urbanministry.org

- worldvision.org

4

Honoring the Poor

How Best to Serve Those in Need

> "We may forget that the poor are not an abstraction but rather a group of human beings who have names, who are made in the image of God, whose hairs are numbered, and for whom Jesus died."[1]
>
> — Bryant Myers, author

start> Group Interaction

> Get Connected   1 minute

Have someone in the group read aloud this brief description of the session theme.

There are approximately 6.9 billion people in the world today, and more than three billion of them — close to half — live on less than two dollars a day. It's an overwhelming statistic, reflective of an overwhelming problem — namely, that too many people are forced to survive on too few resources. "The poor will *always* be with us," overwhelmed hearts insist. "The best efforts will *still* be in vain." It's an understandable posture to assume, but it comes at a terribly high cost.

Jesus' idea when he sent out his disciples — and you — to reach the world with his message of grace was that they would *put off* their selfish concerns and sinful desires and *put on* compassion for a broken and needy world. Following him would mean following the example that he set — feeding hungry people, clothing people who crave warmth, and providing resources to people who are poor.

The stakes were high when Jesus issued his plea. They remain sky-high today, especially for those who call the United States of America home. More than 300 million people live in the U.S., which is less than 6 percent of the world's population. And yet Americans possess a staggering *half* of the world's wealth. "From the one who has been entrusted with much," Jesus promised in Luke 12:48, "much more will be asked."

You've likely been entrusted with much. And a need-laden world is waiting to see if you will be Christ to them. Poverty is real, and its devastating effects are seen on all sides. Your actions matter. Your choices matter. Choose today to **start>**.

> *"Speak up for those who cannot speak for themselves, for*
> *the rights of all who are destitute. Speak up and judge fairly;*
> *defend the rights of the poor and needy."*
>
> — Proverbs 31:8 – 9

Know Your Neighbor   2 minutes

Using one or two words, share your current beliefs or assumptions about the session theme.

What do the poor have to offer the rest of society?

Give Your Heart and Mind to God   1 minute

Addressing the needs of those trapped in cyclical poverty first must begin with genuine submission to the King of compassion, Jesus Christ. Ask God to tenderize your heart to the stories, the facts, and the realities that will be presented in this session's DVD segment. And then request wisdom for knowing how to respond — personally, genuinely, and with great passion for those who are poor.

> Learn Together   30 minutes

If you'd like to take a few notes as you watch the session 4 video segment, use the space below.

> Discuss "Honoring the Poor"   15 minutes

You may not have time to discuss all of the questions in this section — that's okay! Cover as many as you can, thoughtfully, thoroughly, and with great attentiveness.

1. If you were to whittle down the population of planet Earth to precisely one hundred people, with all existing human ratios remaining the same, then based on today's trends the demographics would look like this:

   ❑ The village would have 60 Asians, 14 Africans, 12 Europeans, 8 Latin Americans, 5 from the USA and Canada, and 1 from the South Pacific

   ❑ 51 would be male, 49 would be female

   ❑ 82 would be non-white; 18 white

   ❑ 67 would be people of other religions or no religion; 33 would be Christian

   ❑ 80 would live in substandard housing

   ❑ 67 would be unable to read

- ❑ 50 would be malnourished and 1 dying of starvation
- ❑ 33 would be without access to a safe water supply
- ❑ 39 would lack access to improved sanitation
- ❑ 24 would not have any electricity, and of the 76 that do have electricity, most would only use it for light at night
- ❑ 7 would have access to the Internet
- ❑ 1 would have a college education
- ❑ 1 would have HIV
- ❑ 2 would be near birth; 1 near death
- ❑ 33 would be receiving — and attempting to live on — only 3 percent of the income of "the village"
- ❑ 5 would control 32 percent of the entire village's wealth; all 5 would be U.S. citizens[2]

Which of the sixteen realities noted above surprise you the most? Checkmark the items in the list that apply, and discuss with the group your reasons for selecting each one. Then discuss the remaining questions.

The last statistic hints at the idea that geography plays a significant role in whether or not a person will experience a life lived in poverty. What other factors do you believe inform whether a person lives life poor?

If 33 people would be receiving and attempting to live on only 3 percent of the income of the village, what would you imagine the role of the other 67 percent to be in helping to alleviate the suffering?

Has your understanding of the role of that 67 percent group shifted throughout your life? If so, what experiences have shaped your current understanding?

2. According to the video segment, Steve Chalke realized from the moment he surrendered his life to Jesus Christ that the gospel is good news — socially and emotionally and physically, as *well* as spiritually. Based on your unique personality, predispositions, and life experiences, which of those four areas of faith does your life tend to reflect? Select any that apply from the list below.

   ❏ Social > "I practice and encourage moral and ethical behavior."

   ❏ Emotional > "Through words and sometimes deeds, I encourage peace of mind and heart."

   ❏ Physical > "I invest significant time and energy providing food and clothing to people in need."

   ❏ Spiritual > "I pray for people living far from God, for their salvation and for the living out of their life's purpose."

   As you consider the area(s) of faith you selected, think about what assumptions or experiences play into how faith most often is made manifest in your life. For example, perhaps the church you grew up in placed great emphasis on prayer meetings but never engaged in extending practical compassion to people who were underresourced in your community. As a result, from an early age your faith seemed to bend more toward spiritual reflection than physical action. Jot down your thoughts in the space below, and then share with the group an example or two that came to mind.

3. As it relates to easing the burden of people living in poverty, Steve Chalke said that we grow only as we serve others. How have you found this pattern to be true or untrue in your own life? Explain your answer.

4. If *serving God by serving others* indeed is the goal of the Christ-follower's life, then what attitudes or actions do you believe help move a person along the continuum below toward a lifestyle of service? Note your group's ideas on the lines provided.

$$\dashrightarrow$$

"Taking in" information/
amassing knowledge
about poverty

"Giving out" service/
helping to resource people
who are poor

_____

_____

_____

_____

_____

5. When God's people act on behalf of people who are hungry or oppressed, there is a benefit not only to the recipient of that care, but also to the one who acts. Read Isaiah 58:9b – 12 below and circle the three actions you find in the first sentence of the passage.

    If you do away with the yoke of oppression, with the pointing finger and malicious talk, and if you spend yourselves in behalf of the hungry and satisfy the needs of the oppressed, then your light will rise in the darkness, and your night will become like the noonday. The LORD will guide you always; he will satisfy your needs in a sun-scorched land and will strengthen your frame. You will be like a well-watered garden, like a spring whose waters never fail. Your people will rebuild the ancient ruins and will raise up the age-old foundations; you will be called Repairer of Broken Walls, Restorer of Streets with Dwellings.

    According to the rest of the passage, what are the promises God made to his people if they would take action on behalf of the poor? Fill in the grid below as a group, sharing your thoughts about the meaning behind a few of the promises you find. The first promise has been filled in for you.

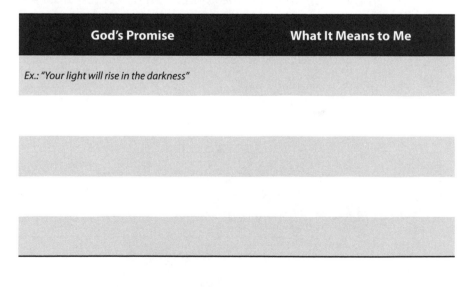

God's Promise	What It Means to Me
Ex.: "Your light will rise in the darkness"	

> **Now Is the Time** 10 minutes

This is the most important part of the session — how your small group will put faith into action. Make each other accountable for starting today!

No matter your story, you have something to offer this hurting world. To illustrate that point, stand with your other group members in a straight line in your meeting room for the "Privilege" exercise, found on pages 92 – 94. After the movement portion of the exercise, remain in your final position and note where you are standing, compared to the position of your group members. Afterward, answer the following questions together.

What are your general observations after completing the exercise?

Which aspects of the exercise were most uncomfortable for you and why?

Did any of the questions cause you to feel devalued in any way? If so, why?

How did your environment or the other group members influence your response to this activity?

What takeaways from this exercise do you hope to carry with you in days to come?

> Close with Prayer

The end of this time together is really the beginning of enormous Good Samaritan possibility for you and your group. Take a moment to offer a prayer of thanksgiving and commitment to God, such as the one that follows.

Creator God,

Thank you for the poor you have placed in my midst. Their presence is a blessing to my soul. I am honored to be able to help them in small ways; I desire to do more. Their fragile lives, coupled with their great faith, are an inspiration and a mystery to me. I want to penetrate their world, share their hope, and learn their secrets. Is it possible that you have placed these people around me to heighten my vulnerability? Is my insensitivity so great that in my arrogance I have confused ownership with security? Is it possible that only the poor possess the keys to your kingdom? Their faces shine with hope and their eyes are radiant with acceptance. Their prayers inspire compassion. You desire that we all might have life and have it abundantly. I now understand that the abundant life is not a material one, but a life of trust in your providence. Guide me to the light of trust. Send the poor to my doorstep that I might learn from them. Bless all those that have less than I do and stir within me the spirit of sharing. Let gratitude and giving be my banners and let all the glory be yours. May justice and mercy have places of honor within my being and may my hands work to relieve suffering wherever I find it. Amen.

—Vera Salter, *A Prayer for the Poor*

start⟩ Personal Reflection

Living out your faith in real and tangible ways is more than just a six-week curriculum — it is a lifelong journey. The "Personal Reflection" section is your "diary" and "guide" as you go forward on this quest. Of course, like any journey, this one will be easier and more fruitful with the support and encouragement of others. **JustStart.org** *is that community. There you'll find other stories and testimonies just like yours, links to organizations and people who need your help and special skills, and opportunities to Learn, Live, and Lead a Good Samaritan lifestyle.*

To reconnect with this session's topic as you dive into the three-part "On Your Own" section, answer the questions below, which reference the DVD material you viewed during your small group time.

1   2   3

1. **Mike Yankoski** said that one of the most meaningful deeds a stranger could do for people who are poor is simply to notice them, to treat them as human beings. Have you ever considered the simple act of "noticing someone" to be a good deed? When have you felt "noticed" by a stranger, and how did the eye contact or words or actions make you feel? Record your responses in the space below.

2. **Steve Chalke** said that if Christians are faithful to get involved in the lives of people who are poor — learning their stories, tending to their hearts, meeting their needs — their lives naturally will have evangelistic impact. In other words, when you feed someone who is hungry, God's love undeniably shines through. Have you found this dynamic to be true in your own life? If so, note an experience below.

3. **Shane Claiborne** encouraged Christ-followers to find their "Calcutta," whether that looks like a slum in India or a home for elderly people down the street from where you live. Based on what you've experienced in this curriculum so far, how would you describe the "Calcutta" where God might be calling you to serve?

> **On Your Own**|START LEARNING

Matthew Parris, writer for London's *The Sunday Times*, issued a plea to local churches to step in where other well-intentioned agencies cannot. The following is an excerpt from "As an Atheist, I Truly Believe Africa Needs God," which ran on 27 December 2008.

Now a confirmed atheist, I've become convinced of the enormous contribution that Christian evangelism makes in Africa: sharply distinct from the work of secular

NGOs [non-governmental organizations], government projects and international aid efforts. These alone will not do. Education and training alone will not do. In Africa Christianity changes people's hearts. It brings a spiritual transformation. The rebirth is real. The change is good.

[When I was young] we had friends who were missionaries, and as a child I stayed often with them; I also stayed, alone with my little brother, in a traditional African village. In the city we had working for us Africans who had converted and were strong believers. The Christians were always different. Far from having cowed to or confined its converts, their faith appeared to have liberated and relaxed them. There was a **liveliness***, a* **curiosity***, an* **engagement** *with the world — a directness in their dealings with others — that seemed to be missing in traditional African life. They stood tall.*

Those who want Africa to walk tall amid 21st-century global competition must not kid themselves that providing the material means or even the knowhow that accompanies what we call development will make the change. A whole belief system must first be supplanted."[3] *(emphasis added)*

Parris makes the statement that poverty is more a spiritual issue than a material one. In what ways might this assertion be true?

In your estimation, why would God leave it up to the church to help solve societal ills?

Parris notes three characteristics of the Christians he came across in the African village of his youth. How would you define each of them as they relate to serving the poor?

- Liveliness

- Curiosity

- Engagement

How well do liveliness, curiosity, and engagement characterize your own attitudes and actions toward the poor?

As you scan the "Learn" opportunities below, ask God to forge greater longing to serve people in your midst who are less resourced than you. Select whichever one catches your eye to implement this week, and see what God might do!

LEARN   ●○○

● **How rich are you, really?** Visit the Global Rich List — globalrichlist.com — and see where you rank on the list of the world's wealthiest people.

● **Explore homelessness.** Read and meditate on the excerpt from Mike Yankoski's book, *Under the Overpass*, found on pages 90 – 91. What thoughts or convictions swirl in your mind and heart as you sit with his words? Where does Jesus' claim in Matthew 5:3 ("blessed are the poor in spirit") intersect the themes of Mike's writing?

● **Write God's Word on your heart.** Memorize a portion of verses in Acts 2 – 4. Among the early church communities, no one was in need. Who is in need in your family or on your block? What resources could you share with them today?

● **Join forces with your church.** Check with your local church to find out what God is already doing to serve those with tremendous need in your community. How might God be prompting you to join forces in alleviating suffering?

> **On Your Own**|START LIVING IT OUT

In this session's video segment, John Ortberg mentioned five clarifications of what it means to be "rich toward God." Which of his definitions most accurately characterizes your life today?

Select one from the following list:

- ❑ A soul that is increasingly healthy and good
- ❑ The propensity for loving and enjoying the people in my life
- ❑ The tendency to use my passions to do good in the world
- ❑ A generous spirit regarding my material possessions and other resources
- ❑ The practice of forcing the "temporary" to submit to that which is eternal

Which one represents the greatest challenge for you to live out, and why? Write your response below.

What is one attitude or action you can shift in order to grow in the area you noted?

Throughout Scripture God is known by many roles, such as Provider, Companion, Encourager, and Friend. Fill in the blank below with the role which would be most helpful to you as you seek to accomplish that growth.

God, be my _____ today.

Before moving on, jot down your own version of Psalm 37:16 on the lines below as a prayer to God for wisdom and inspiration to begin living in a way that is considered "rich" toward him.

"Better the little that the righteous have than the wealth of many wicked..."

—Psalm 37:16

_____

_____

_____

_____

CHECKING IN

Think back on the "Privilege" exercise (pages 92–94) from your group time this week, and note your thoughts in response to the following questions:

How do you recall feeling upon completing the exercise?

How might God want to transform those feelings and emotions into action on behalf of the poor?

Which item from the "Live It Out" list on the next page could give you a place to start? Select one and begin today!

LIVE IT OUT ○●○

- **Leverage a line.** While you are waiting in line at the grocery store or the coffee shop, strike up a conversation with the person next to you simply to find a way to encourage them in the moment. Offer to cover their bill if you are so moved.

- **Opt for cash only.** Citibank has determined that consumers will spend 26 percent more money if they are carrying a credit card rather than cash. For seven days straight, adopt a cash-only policy and journal the insights you glean.

- **Scour your street.** Interview the five people who live closest to your home in order to uncover as many needs as possible. Who is a single mom? Who just lost his job? Who needs help caring for disabled children or aging parents? Who is in terrible debt? Journal what you learn about the people living near you, and ask God to guide you toward meeting one of those needs.

- **Care for a child.** Sponsor a child through an organization like World Vision (world vision.org). Make an individual commitment, or consider sponsoring one or two children along with your friends or small group members.

- **Provide tools for schools.** Support children and families through World Vision's efforts to equip and empower underresourced communities across the nation. Participate in the SchoolTools™ program and help remove roadblocks to education by collecting essential school supplies and assembling kits for children in need. For more information, visit worldvision.org/start.

- **Have ears to hear and hands that give.** This week, when you see someone who may be homeless, take the time to share a meal or coffee in order to hear their story. If that seems to be too far outside your comfort zone, offer up a gift card from a nearby fast-food restaurant so that they can experience the dignity of selecting and purchasing lunch on their own.

"The great tragedy of the church is not that rich people do not care about the poor but that rich people do not know the poor."

— Shane Claiborne, author and activist

> **On Your Own** | START LEADING

Steve Chalke said that a Jesus-centered faith, according to Matthew 22:37 – 39, is defined as a "faith that loves God and loves our neighbor as ourselves."

> Do you believe that it's possible to have one without the other: can you love God without loving others? Can you love others without loving God? What beliefs or assumptions inform your answers? Note them in the space below.

> Who in your life seems to exemplify an all-encompassing faith by loving God and loving others equally well?

> What words of encouragement could you offer to that person as a way of saying thanks for his or her example in your life? Write down those words in the space below, and then convey them to that person this week!

> As you close your "On Your Own" time today, read the "Lead" opportunities that follow, noting the one(s) God prompts you to try.

LEAD ○○●

● **Try friend raising!** Rather than raising funds, try your hand at "friend raising." Share your passion for serving the poor with people in your sphere of influence, and challenge them to serve alongside you this week.

● **Take inventory.** After evaluating the excess electronics around your home, offer gently used cameras, televisions, computers, and other pieces of equipment to an area agency or a school in an impoverished neighborhood, then volunteer your services to help the children, teachers, or staff learn basic operating skills.

● **Be a voice for the voiceless.** Invite your small group to join you in writing a letter to your city council, mayor, or congressperson addressing an area of concern for under-resourced people in your community.

● **Host a 30 Hour Famine.** Bring World Vision's 30 Hour Famine™ to your church's youth group and help them grow closer to Christ while they engage in an international movement to fight hunger. They'll fast for thirty hours while raising funds to feed and care for children around the world. The spiritual discipline of fasting, combined with learning about world hunger and serving the poor, will deepen their understanding of their place in the world as Christians — and they'll have a blast hanging out with their friends, playing the interactive TRIBE game, and engaging in local service projects. To sign up, visit 30hourfamine.org.

● **Work at "McDonald's."** Have two hours and in the mood for some fun? Gather a group of six to eight people to buy groceries and prepare meals at your local Ronald McDonald House. Visit rmhc.com for details.

● **Grab your hammer and a few friends.** Join your small group or colleagues from work in assisting with a Habitat for Humanity build this weekend. Habitat builds simple, decent, and affordable houses for low-income families. Browsing habitat.org is a great way to start.

● **Experience poverty ... for real.** Ready for a unique opportunity to see the world through different eyes? Check out Mission Waco's weekend-long "Poverty Simulation" at missionwaco.org for details on how to experience what impoverished people walk through every single day.

start⟩ *Ready for More?*

⟩ **Read**

- *Different Eyes: The Art of Living Beautifully*, Steve Chalke (Zondervan)

- *Zealous Love: A Practical Guide to Social Justice*, Mike and Danae Yankoski (Zondervan)

- *Under the Overpass: A Journey of Faith on the Streets of America*, Mike Yankoski (Zondervan)

- *Churches That Make a Difference: Reaching Your Community with Good News and Good Works*, Ronald Sider, Philip Olson, and Heidi Unruh (Baker)

- *Walking with the Poor: Principles and Practices of Transformational Development*, Bryant L. Myers (Orbis)

- *A Heart for the Community: New Models for Urban and Suburban Ministry*, John Fuder and Noel Castellanos (Moody)

- *Ministries of Mercy*, Timothy J. Keller (P & R)

- *The Poor Will Be Glad*, Peter Greer and Phil Smith (Zondervan)

- *The Compassion Revolution: How God Can Use You to Meet the World's Greatest Needs*, Dave Donaldson (Harvest House)

- *Make Poverty Personal: Taking the Poor as Seriously as the Bible Does*, Ash Barker (Baker)

- *When Helping Hurts: How to Alleviate Poverty without Hurting the Poor … and Yourself*, Steve Corbett and Brian Fikkert (Moody)

- *Beyond Charity: The Call to Christian Community Development*, John Perkins (Baker)

> Watch

- *City of God* (O2 Films, 2002, rated "R")

- *Slumdog Millionaire* (Celador Films, 2009, rated "R")

- *The Grapes of Wrath* (Twentieth Century Fox Film Corporation, 1940, not rated)

> Surf

- juststart.org

- worldvision.org

- one.org

- compassion.com

- bread.org

- ccda.org (Christian Community Development Association)

- hopeinternational.com

- wfp.org (World Food Programme)

- putyourfaithinaction.org

- feedthechildren.org

Excerpt from *Under the Overpass*

by Mike Yankoski

The idea had dropped into my brain one Sunday morning while I sat in church. The pastor was delivering a powerful sermon about living the Christian life. The gist of it was, "Be the Christian you say you are." Suddenly I was shocked to realize that I had just driven twenty minutes past the world that needed me to be the Christian I say I am, in order to hear a sermon entitled, "Be the Christian You Say You Are." Soon I would drive back past that same world to the privilege of my comfortable life on campus at a Christian college.

Thinking ahead to the following week, I knew several things would happen. I knew I'd hear more lectures about being a caring Christian or living a godly life. I'd read more books about who God is and about what the world needs now. I'd spend more time late at night down at a coffee shop with my friends, kicking around ultimate questions and finely delivered opinions about the world.

Then I'd jump into my warm bed and turn out the light. Another day gone.

But we were created to be and to do, not merely to discuss. The hypocrisy in my life troubled me. No, I wasn't in the grip of rampant sin, but at the same time, for the life of me I couldn't find a connecting thread of radical, living obedience between what I *said* about my world and how I *lived* in it. Sure, I claimed that Christ was my stronghold, my peace, my sustenance, my joy. But I did all that from the safety of my comfortable upper-middle-class life. I never really had to put my claims to the test.

I sat there in church struggling to remember a time when I'd actually needed to lean fully on Christ rather than on my own abilities. Not much came to mind. What was Paul's statement in Philippians? "I have learned what it means to be content in all circumstances, whether with everything or with nothing" (4:11 – 12, author's abridgment).

With nothing?

The idea came instantly — like the flash of a camera or a flicker of lightning. It left me breathless, and it changed my life. *What if I stepped out of my comfortable life with nothing but God and put my faith to the test alongside of those who live with nothing every day?*

The picture that came with that question was of me homeless and hungry on the streets of an American city.

Hard on the heels of the idea came the questions: What if I didn't actually believe the things I argued with so much certainty? What, for example, if I didn't truly believe that Christ is my identity, my strength, my hope? Or worse, what if I leaped in faith, but God didn't catch me? My mind reeled.

And then there were the practical questions. Could I survive on the streets? How much did I really want to learn to be content *always* with *nothing*? What would my friends think? What would my parents think? My pastors? My professors? Would I be okay? What if I got sick? What if I starved? What if I got beat up? What if I froze?

What if I'm wrong?

Am I crazy?

Will I die?

But already, I had decided. I walked out of church that morning seized by a big idea, assaulted by dozens of questions, and sure that I had heard deep in my heart a still, small voice saying, "Follow Me."[4]

Privilege Exercise[5]

Objective

To assist group members in seeing and feeling the inequities many people face in our world today.

Activity

DIRECTIONS: Line up with your group members in a straight line across the room. Your group leader will read a list of thirty-six statements; at the end of each statement, follow the direction given if the statement applies to you. [NOTE: If your entire group is socioeconomically homogenous, select half of the group members to respond in **opposite** fashion to each of the thirty-six statements, so that in the end the group will see the disparity that surfaces among the general population.]

1. If your ancestors were forced to come to the USA (not by choice), take one step back.

2. If your primary ethnic identity is American, take one step forward.

3. If you were ever called names because of your race, class, ethnicity, or gender, take one step back.

4. If there were people of color who worked in your household as servants, housekeepers, gardeners, etc., take one step forward.

5. If you were often embarrassed or ashamed of your clothes, house, car, etc., take one step back.

6. If either of your parents was a "professional"—doctor, lawyer, executive, etc.—take one step forward.

7. If you were raised in an area where there was prostitution, drug activity, etc., take one step back.

8. If you ever tried to change your appearance, mannerisms, or behavior to avoid being judged or ridiculed, take one step back.

9. If you studied the culture of your ancestors in elementary school, take one step forward.

10. If you went to school speaking a language other than English, take one step back.

11. If there were more than fifty books in your house when you grew up, take one step forward.

12. If you ever had to skip a meal or were hungry when you were growing up because there was not enough money to buy food, take one step back.

13. If your parents took you to art galleries or plays, take one step forward.

14. If one of your parents was unemployed or laid off (not by choice), take one step back.

15. If you attended a private school or summer camp, take one step forward.

16. If your family ever had to move because they could not afford the rent, take one step back.

17. If you were told that you were beautiful, smart, and capable by your parents, take one step forward.

18. If you were ever discouraged from academic participation or jobs because of race, class, ethnicity, or gender, take one step back.

19. If you were encouraged to attend college by your parents, take one step forward.

20. If prior to age 18 you took a vacation out of the country, take one step forward.

21. If one of your parents did not complete high school, take one step back.

22. If your family owned their own home, take one step forward.

23. If you saw members of your race, ethnic group, or gender portrayed on television in degrading roles, take one step back.

24. If you were ever offered a good job because of your association with a friend or family member, take one step forward.

25. If you were ever denied employment because of your race, ethnicity, or gender, take one step back.

26. If you were paid less, treated less fairly because of race, ethnicity, or gender, take one step back.

27. If you were ever accused of cheating or lying because of your race, ethnicity, or gender, take one step back.

28. If you ever inherited money or property, take one step forward.

29. If you had to rely primarily on public transportation growing up, take one step back.

30. If you were ever stopped or questioned by the police because of your race, ethnicity, or gender, take one step back.

31. If you were ever afraid of violence because of your race, ethnicity, or gender, take one step back.

32. If you were generally able to avoid places that were dangerous, take one step forward.

33. If you ever felt uncomfortable about a joke related to your race, ethnicity, or gender, take one step back.

34. If you were ever the victim of violence related to your race, ethnicity, or gender, take one step back.

35. If your parents did not grow up in the United States, take one step back.

36. If your parents told you that you could be anything you wanted to be, take one step forward.

Tending to God's Creation

Why Environmental Stewardship Is Biblical and Beneficial

5

> "I often hear people tell me that they don't think that their individual efforts can make a difference. But the truth is that every action makes a difference. We just need to start."[1]
>
> — Thomas Kostigen, *author*

start> Group Interaction

> Get Connected

1 minute

Have someone in the group read aloud this brief description of the session theme.

In Genesis 2:15, God placed a man in the Garden of Eden to "work it and take care of it." Despite the clarity of that phrase, many Christ-followers today live as though they exist on a disposable planet and behave as though they will never be called to account for how they steward the gift of God's physical world.

But hope is still alive. As you dive into the subject of creation care, open your heart and your mind to the ways in which we as Christians who love and serve Christ can shape our personal lives in creation-friendly ways by conserving resources and practicing creation-friendly habits. And be encouraged as you experience afresh the joy of connecting with the natural world God himself formed.

Your actions matter. Your choices matter. Choose today to **start>**.

"The earth is the Lord's, and everything in it."

—Psalm 24:1

❯ Know Your Neighbor

2 minutes

Using one or two words, share your current beliefs or assumptions about the session theme.

What one word comes to mind when you hear the term "environmentalist"?

❯ Give Your Heart and Mind to God

1 minute

Creation care can be a tricky topic to discuss in Christian circles because for many people, the issue holds significant political and societal associations. As you begin your group time, resubmit your mind and heart to the authority of God. Invite him to move and stir as his Spirit pleases. Ask him to remove all distractions — ambient noise in your meeting space, the day's demands, tomorrow's concerns … as well as preconceived ideas about the topic of creation care — and to calm your soul as you experience session 5.

❯ Learn Together

30 minutes

If you'd like to take a few notes as you watch the session 5 video segment, use the space below.

❯ Discuss "Tending to God's Creation" 20 minutes

You may not have time to discuss all of the questions in this section — that's okay! Cover as many as you can, thoughtfully, thoroughly, and with great attentiveness.

1. Think back on the assumptions aired by your group at the beginning of this session. How were they validated or challenged by the DVD content? Note your response in the space below before sharing it with your group.

2. During the video segment, Session teacher Matthew Sleeth made the comment, "There are now no elms on Elm Street, no chestnuts left on Chestnut Street, and no caribou left in Caribou, Maine." In your own surroundings, how do you see evidence of environmental change? Record your group's input on any shifts that you collectively see in the natural world elements represented by the image below, such as air quality, wildlife, plant life, and water sources.

Changes we see include:

3. Read the words of Psalm 65:8 – 13 below, and then answer the questions that follow.

The whole earth is filled with awe at your wonders; where morning dawns, where evening fades, you call forth songs of joy. You care for the land and water it; you enrich it abundantly. The streams of God are filled with water to provide the people with grain, for so you have ordained it. You drench its furrows and level its ridges; you soften it with showers and bless its crops. You crown the year with your bounty, and your carts overflow with abundance. The grasslands of the wilderness overflow; the hills are clothed with gladness. The meadows are covered with flocks and the valleys are mantled with grain; they shout for joy and sing.

What do you believe is the Christ-follower's role in ensuring that "grasslands overflow," and that "hills are clothed with gladness" in this generation and in generations to come? Write down your thoughts in the space below before sharing them with your group.

How does the "dominion" that humankind was given in the Genesis account relate to life today? In other words, what does having "dominion … over all the earth" and all of the creatures in it (Genesis 1:26 KJV) mean practically for a stay-at-home parent or a busy business owner or a teen who is about to graduate from high school? Discuss your thoughts with your group, jotting down themes that surface in the space below.

4. Most people would agree that they feel good about themselves when they faithfully take care of something that belongs to someone else. Think back on times when you have experienced the rewards of stewardship. What were the items or situations or people you were entrusted to care for, what motivated you to exhibit good steward-ship, and what were the results? Fill in the grid below as recollections come to mind, and be prepared to share one or two examples with your group. A sample entry has been provided to get you started.

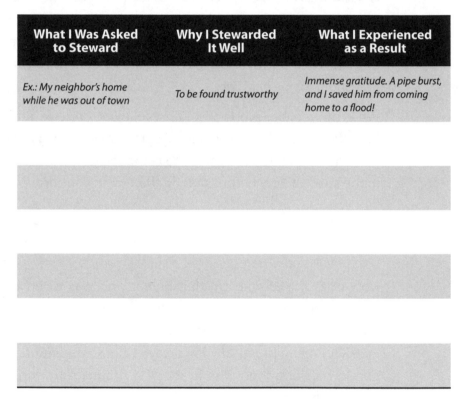

What I Was Asked to Steward	Why I Stewarded It Well	What I Experienced as a Result
Ex.: My neighbor's home while he was out of town	*To be found trustworthy*	*Immense gratitude. A pipe burst, and I saved him from coming home to a flood!*

Take a look at the information you wrote down on the grid on page 100. What thoughts or realizations come to mind as you reflect on those experiences now? Share one or two of them with your group.

> Now Is the Time   5 minutes

This is the most important part of the session — how your small group will put faith into action. Make each other accountable for starting today!

We've come to rely on (and love) technology. Take a few minutes to brainstorm as a group appliances and electronic gadgets you didn't own five to ten years ago that you "couldn't live without" today. Then select one appliance or piece of electronic equipment — such as your dishwasher, your clothes dryer, your iPod, or your TV — and suspend use of it from now until your group meets again. Partway through your experience, flip to the Journal section of this guide that begins on page 149 and record your responses to the following questions:

1. What emotions are you experiencing as you voluntarily deny yourself a modern convenience?

2. What are the most frustrating or challenging aspects of the experiment? What are the most beneficial or rewarding ones?

3. What observations are you making about yourself along the way? About God? About your lifestyle as you know it?

> Close with Prayer

The end of this time together is really the beginning of enormous Good Samaritan possibility for you and your group. Take a moment to offer a prayer of thanksgiving and commitment to God, such as the one that follows.

> *This world*
> *Your creation*
> *Rolled into a sphere*
> *Packaged in sunshine*
> *Gift-wrapped in love*
> *Given to us*
> *Thank you*
>
> — *Prayer on the Theme of Creation,*
> Celtic Christian Church[2]

start⟩ Personal Reflection

Living out your faith in real and tangible ways is more than just a six-week curriculum—it is a lifelong journey. The "Personal Reflection" section is your "diary" and "guide" as you go forward on this quest. Of course, like any journey, this one will be easier and more fruitful with the support and encouragement of others. **JustStart.org** *is that community. There you'll find other stories and testimonies just like yours, links to organizations and people who need your help and special skills, and opportunities to Learn, Live, and Lead a Good Samaritan lifestyle.*

To reconnect with this session's topic as you dive into the three-part "On Your Own" section, answer the questions below, which reference the DVD material you viewed during your small group time.

1. Emergency-room-doctor-turned-environmentalist **Matthew Sleeth** mentioned that he's rarely heard the terms "tree-hugger" and "Christian" used lovingly in the same sentence. Why do you suppose a negative connotation has existed in evangelical circles regarding people who are environmental advocates? Record your thoughts in the space below.

2. **Shirley Mullen**, president of Houghton College, said that "creation care requires faithfulness to new habits, and faithfulness is not something that any of us is very good at by ourselves." In the space

below, jot down the names of two or three people who might be willing to explore a few new creation care habits. Choose one of them to tell about your "appliance ban" and journal discoveries.

3. At the beginning of the DVD portion for this session, host **John Ortberg** said that Christ-followers must remember that the earth belongs to God. "God says, 'Here, I'm going to give you the keys,'" John said, "'but remember, it's not yours. You may not abuse it. Instead, bring it to its fullest potential.'" On the lines below, describe what you imagine the earth would look like, once it's brought to its "fullest potential."

- _____
- _____
- _____
- _____

> **On Your Own** | START LEARNING

A 2008 National Geographic Society article titled, "One River at a Time," featured the story of an unsuspecting environmentalist named Chad Pregracke. Take a look at the excerpt below and on the next page, then answer the questions that follow.

> *All Chad Pregracke meant to do was pick up some of the trash littering the bottom of the Mississippi River, where he spent so much of his childhood. Eleven years and 54,360 bags of trash later, Pregracke's one-man effort in East Moline, Illinois, has turned into a major undertaking; his nonprofit Living Lands and Waters now organizes cleanups along six other rivers in the Northeast and Midwest. By the end of last year, his volunteers had cleared 497 tons of metal; 52,195 tires; 1,433 major appliances, and enough polystyrene foam to cover ten football fields. You may not be able to devote your life to river cleanups, but even spending an afternoon clean-*

ing the shores of a lake, beach, or river near you can be just as satisfying and has a significant environmental impact. And Chad will have a lot less trash to pick up the next time he's in town.[3]

Based on the story you just read, where would you rank yourself in terms of activism compared to someone like Chad? Place an "X" on the line below.

The guy is crazy!   I'm not *quite* as   Chad and I are cut from
                                 motivated at that   the same cloth

Even if you're not prone to cleaning out an entire river, you too probably have a few "conservation-minded" parts of your life. Considering your present lifestyle, in which areas are you a conservationist and in which ones are you more extravagant — or careless, even? Note your responses on the grid below. A couple of examples have been provided to get you started.

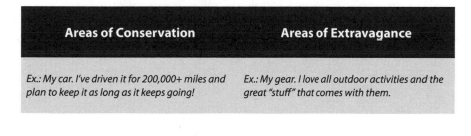

Areas of Conservation	Areas of Extravagance
Ex.: My car. I've driven it for 200,000+ miles and plan to keep it as long as it keeps going!	*Ex.: My gear. I love all outdoor activities and the great "stuff" that comes with them.*

As you review the grid you completed on page 105, what insights come to mind regarding areas where you're honoring God and his creation and areas where you might need to adjust your behavior? Discuss your thoughts with your group at an upcoming meeting.

Session teacher Matthew Sleeth referenced the fact that as an ER doctor, he insisted that his patients wishing to start a diet first weigh-in so that they would know the truth of their present condition. In the spirit of knowing the truth about *your* life — as well as increasing awareness about the waste you create and the energy you use — complete the energy audit found on pages 117 – 118. Then, answer the questions below.

Which of your audit results surprised you? Which ones validated what you already sensed about your lifestyle? Note your insights below.

It is reported that since 1960 the amount of waste produced by Americans has almost *doubled*, from 2.7 pounds to 4.6 pounds per day.[4] How might an *increase in awareness* of the waste that you create fuel an *increase in care* for the world that God made?

If you're ready to raise your awareness in the area of creation care, skim the list of "Learn" opportunities below, noting one or two items that reflect the most reasonable way for you to start to care for creation today. Then, take steps to complete them in the next few days.

LEARN ●○○

● **Count your stuff.** On average, an American possesses *ten thousand* things. Determine where you are compared to the national average by counting your possessions. (You might try tackling just one room first! And yes, a pair of shoes can count as one "thing.")

● **Consider yourself a steward.** Make a list of your favorite "possessions" and record your ideas about how they might be used to impact the kingdom. How might your life look different if you truly believed that every resource you "possess" is really a gift from God to be stewarded well? Journal your thoughts.

● **See what Scripture says.** Visit creation-care.org to find out what the Bible says about stewarding planet Earth. Jot down a meaningful verse on a card that you keep on the fridge, your bathroom mirror, or your dashboard.

● **Create a book circle.** Invite a few friends to read *Serve God, Save the Planet* by Matthew Sleeth or *You Are Here* by Thomas Kostigen. Notice themes that surface during your discussions and take note of ideas that seem doable within the group.

● **Google greenish things.** Google communities such as *Jesus People, USA* in Chicago; *Communality* in Lexington, Kentucky; and *A Simple Way* in Philadelphia. What are some of the aspects of community that pique your interest? List some of the personal sacrifices that are made in order to live in community.

● **Pray a green passage.** Reference *The Green Bible* by visiting greenletterbible.com to glean creation care insights from leaders such as Desmond Tutu, Brian McLaren, Matthew Sleeth, and N. T. Wright. Verses related to stewardship of God's creation are highlighted in green. Spend a few minutes praying a "green" passage back to God; record insights that he impresses on your mind and heart in the Journal section of this guide, which begins on page 149.

● **Get in touch with your artistic side.** Read the lyrics to the hymn, "This Is My Father's World" (see page 108). Journal your thoughts about the words to the song. Also, consider how art can affect your lifestyle — and specifically your interest in creation care.

● **Have a candid conversation.** Discuss with a friend or family member how your resources might be impacting your world positively and which ones might be having a negative effect. Consider resources such as your finances, your time, your car, your house, your trash, your energy use, and so forth.

This Is My Father's World

This is my Father's world, and to my listening ears
all nature sings, and round me rings the music of the spheres.
This is my Father's world: I rest me in the thought
of rocks and trees, of skies and seas; his hand the wonders
*   wrought.*
This is my Father's world, the birds their carols raise,
the morning light, the lily white, declare their maker's praise.
This is my Father's world: he shines in all that's fair;
in the rustling grass I hear him pass; he speaks to me every-
*   where.*
This is my Father's world. O let me ne'er forget
that though the wrong seems oft so strong, God is the ruler yet.
This is my Father's world: why should my heart be sad?
The Lord is King; let the heavens ring! God reigns; let the earth
*   be glad!*

—Lyrics by Maltbie D. Babcock (1901)

> On Your Own|START LIVING IT OUT

Envision your favorite place in the world. Maybe it's a beachfront cottage. It might be in the shadow of a snowcapped peak. Or it could be your favorite spot is a room in your very own home. What about that place draws you to it? As insights come to mind, complete the sentences in the grid on the next page.

When I'm there, I see …

What I like to do there is to …

When I'm there, I feel …

Some of my favorite memories there include …

The adjectives that come to mind
when I think about that place now are …

The creation scene described in Genesis, and referred to elsewhere in the Bible, is perhaps the most profound set of activities ever recorded. Find a quiet spot where you can read aloud the passages below. Then answer the questions that follow.

> *You alone are the Lord. You made the heavens, even the highest heavens, and all their starry host, the earth and all that is on it, the seas and all that is in them. You give life to everything, and the multitudes of heaven worship you.*
>
> —Nehemiah 9:6

> *God made the wild animals according to their kinds, the livestock according to their kinds, and all the creatures that move along the ground according to their kinds. And God saw that it was good. Then God said, "Let us make man in our image, in our likeness, and let them rule over the fish of the sea and the birds of the air, over the livestock, over all the earth, and over all the creatures that move along the ground." So God created man in his own image, in the image of God he created him; male and female he created them. God blessed them and said to them, "Be fruitful and increase in number; fill the earth and subdue it. Rule over the fish of the sea and the birds of the air and over every living creature that moves on the ground."*
>
> *Then God said, "I give you every seed-bearing plant on the face of the whole earth and every tree that has fruit with seed in it. They will be yours for food. And to all the beasts of the earth and all the birds of the air and all the creatures that move*

on the ground — everything that has the breath of life in it — I give every green plant for food." And it was so. God saw all that he had made, and it was very good. And there was evening, and there was morning — the sixth day. Thus the heavens and the earth were completed in all their vast array.

— Genesis 1:25 – 2:1 NIV

The LORD God formed the man from the dust of the ground and breathed into his nostrils the breath of life, and the man became a living being. Now the LORD God had planted a garden in the east, in Eden; and there he put the man he had formed. And the LORD God made all kinds of trees grow out of the ground — trees that were pleasing to the eye and good for food.... The LORD God took the man and put him in the Garden of Eden to work it and take care of it.... Now the LORD God had formed out of the ground all the beasts of the field and all the birds of the air. He brought them to the man to see what he would name them; and whatever the man called each living creature, that was its name. So the man gave names to all the livestock, the birds of the air and all the beasts of the field.

— Genesis 2:7 – 9, 15, 19 – 20 NIV

It's possible that the Garden of Eden was God's favorite place on planet Earth. Based on the passages you just read, complete the following sentence starters, this time imagining God's point of view.

In the Garden of Eden, I saw . . .

What I loved to do in Eden was to . . .

When I was in the Garden, I felt . . .

Some of my favorite memories of Eden include . . .

The adjectives that come to mind when I think about life in Eden are . . .

In today's environment, what do you see that you would still declare "good"?

On the flip side of the coin, what aspects of today's natural world give you pause because they seem decidedly "not good"?

How might simplifying your lifestyle, such as by turning off TVs and un-plugging equipment and "streamlining your stuff," create something of a revised Garden of Eden in your own heart for God to occupy?

CHECKING IN

How is your appliance ban going? If you haven't taken a few minutes to record your thoughts and impressions, do it now! Flip back to the session's "Now Is the Time" section on page 101 to refresh your memory on the original challenge.

Now, if you're ready to up the ante on your activity level regarding creation care, take a look at the "Live It Out" opportunities on page 112. What is one thing *you* can do between now and the next time your small group meets?

LIVE IT OUT　○●○

● **Unplug!** Unplug all electronics and power strips when they are not in use to avoid incurring electricity costs for what is called the "phantom load."

● **Unscrew five.** It's said that if everyone changed five light bulbs to energy efficient ones, it would be like taking eight million cars off the road. Give it a try today! Change out five of your most used light bulbs to compact fluorescent bulbs. Visit the EPA energy star website or juststart.org for details.

● **Avoid the junk.** Lessen the junk mail you receive by writing to Mail Preference Service, c/o Direct Marketing Association, PO Box 9008, Farmingdale, NY, 11735 – 9008, or by visiting dmachoice.org. Include the date and a note stating your request to be registered with the Mail Preference Service.

● **Opt for stainless steel.** Switch from plastic, disposable water bottles to a stainless steel option instead.

● **Chill out.** Turn down your heating by five degrees if it's wintertime, or your air conditioner up by five degrees if it is spring or summer. Share the results of your experiment with your friends and family members.

● **Leave the car in the garage.** Use public transportation once this week and record what the experience was like.

● **Eat waste-free.** Pack waste-free lunches for your spouse or children, including reusable utensils, carrying cases, and linen napkins. Journal whether the shift was easy to make or posed unexpected inconveniences.

● **Turn off the tap.** In the time it takes to brush your teeth, you will save almost five gallons of water, which is more water than an average citizen of Kenya uses throughout an entire day.[5] Give it a whirl this week and see how you fare!

● **Recycle!** Grab a box or bin, put it in an out-of-the-way corner, and begin training yourself to think before you discard something in the trash. Combine errands this week and deliver your recyclables when you'll be in that part of town.

● **Shop locally.** Take advantage of nearby farmer's markets, and you'll be supporting your local economy *and* making healthier choices.

● **Dig in the dirt.** Get your hands dirty by planting a garden next spring. Use the herbs and vegetables in your meals and invite friends over to enjoy the bounty. Many groups plant community gardens, which are fun opportunities to socialize, share resources, and forge relationships with neighbors.

● **Compost it!** Instead of shoving food scraps down the food disposer this week, try your hand at composting. Then, use the by-products of your work in your plant or vegetable garden. Visit howtocompost.org or juststart.org for information on how to get going.

"There is no such thing as throwing anything away."

—Thomas Kostigen, *You Are Here*[6]

> **On Your Own** | START LEADING

In session 1, Eugene Peterson reminded you that the religion scholar who provoked Jesus to tell the parable of the Good Samaritan was in fact "looking for a loophole" (Luke 10:29 MSG).

Then, in this session, Matthew Sleeth mentioned that the key point of the Good Samaritan story was not that someone took notice of the man who had been beaten and robbed. The power of the story was that one person finally was willing to get off of his donkey and act.

"There is an old saying: If you are troubled, chop wood and carry water. This is wise advice. If you pray at the same time, so much the better." [7]

— Matthew Sleeth

As it relates to your life today, what "loopholes," excuses, or distractions most threaten to keep you from taking action in the area of creation care? Record your answers below.

On the other hand, consider what it would look like for you to "get off your donkey" and act. Take a look at the five "Lead" suggestions on page 114. Which of these would provide you a healthy challenge this week? Note the ones that apply, and then get busy implementing them!

LEAD ○○●

● **Run the numbers.** Invite two or three friends to view Chris Jordan's photographic art exhibit "Running the Numbers," found online at chrisjordan.com and then discuss your reactions together. Pray for guidance regarding what you as a small band of believers can do to make a difference in your generation.

● **Share and share alike.** Try sharing resources with families on your block. How would co-op babysitting, carpooling, or gardening impact your street, or even your entire neighborhood?

● **Request recycling.** Write letters to your city officials requesting recycling services to your neighborhood. In the meantime, offer to be the "recycling captain" for your block if your neighborhood does not pick up recyclables curbside. Gather and deliver recyclable goods, and then work toward inviting others to share a rotation.

● **Go clean, go green.** Organize a "Clean and Green" day with friends, your neighbors, or another small group of people. Devote the day to cleaning up a church campus, a street, a neighborhood, or a public area such as a park. Organize **start>** groups in your neighborhood! Be the spark that sets your sphere of influence ablaze for issues of creation care.

● **Read and lead.** Read the story below of Mary Margaret Bartley. What is one way that you can encourage your neighborhood to model her approach?

Eight years ago Mary Margaret Bartley and her husband, Stewart, intentionally relocated to the neighborhood of Austin in Chicago, Illinois. Soon after their arrival, they realized that they were surrounded by neighbors who wanted, like them, to honor both God and other people by being better stewards of the world in which they lived.

Before long, the Bartleys and their neighbors had made an informal arrangement to be generous with the everyday resources of life. "It wasn't so much the practical part that compelled us," she explains, "but the overall idea that everything belongs to God, and we are simply called to steward well the things we find in our midst. So far we have a shared Shop-Vac®, a shared table saw, a shared weed-whacker, a shared ladder, a shared lawn mower, and on and on it goes." When asked who foots the bill when the lawn mower has an attitude, she didn't miss a beat. "We pool our money and have it fixed."

The family across the street has two children and one car. They take public transportation as much as possible, but when schedules are especially demanding, neighbors loan them a car. "There are literally dozens of cars that sit unused all day long in this neighborhood. My husband and I both work from home, for example, so there are plenty of times when we don't need ours. We're glad to have friends who can use our resources when we aren't using them, and we treasure that type of cooperation in return."

Mary Margaret acknowledges that an urban setting makes an easier backdrop against which to live out this "shared" lifestyle. But she's quick to remind suburbanites that there are small steps they can take. "Sometimes progress is as simple as walking down the street," she says. "If you have a front porch, sit on it! Host a block party at a local park or in your own backyard — do whatever you need to do to share a meal and a conversation with the people who live nearby. Create room for relationships to be formed, and then just watch what God will do.

"We want to live with open hands," she says, "being good stewards of the resources *and* the relationships that God has entrusted to us." What a gift to their community — and to their God — that decision must be.[8]

start? Ready for More?

> Read

- *The Gospel According to the Earth: Why the Good Book Is a Green Book*, Matthew Sleeth (HarperOne)

- *Saving God's Green Earth: Rediscovering the Church's Responsibility to Environmental Stewardship*, Tri Robinson (Ampelon)

- *For the Beauty of the Earth: A Christian Vision for Creation Care*, Steven Bouma-Prediger (Baker Academic)

- *Green Like God: Unlocking the Divine Plan for Our Planet*, Jonathan Merritt (Faith Words)

> Watch

- *Earth* (Disney Nature, 2009, rated "G")

- *Planet Earth* (BBC Warner, 2007, not rated)

> Surf

- juststart.org

- blessedearth.org

- flourishonline.org

- earthministry.org

- creationcare.org

- energystar.gov

Serve God, Save the Planet Energy Audit[9]

Use your most recent electricity and fuel bills to estimate the following:

Annual kWh of electricity   _____ x .06 = _____

Annual therms or ccf of natural gas   _____ x .88 = _____

Annual gallons of #2 fuel oil   _____ x 1.23 = _____

Annual gallons of propane   _____ x .80 = _____   **– or –**

Annual pounds of propane   _____ x .19 = _____

Annual cords of wood   _____ x 220 = _____

Car 1: _____ divided by _____ x 1 = _____
      miles driven annually   *mpg*

Car 2: _____ divided by _____ x 1 = _____
      miles driven annually   *mpg*

Car 3: _____ divided by _____ x 1 = _____
      miles driven annually   *mpg*

Diesel vehicle:

_____ divided by _____ x 1.23 = _____
      miles driven annually   *mpg*

Miles of airline travel   _____ x .044 = _____

Gallons of gasoline used annually
for boats, mowers, snowmobiles,
chainsaws, ATVs, etc.   _____ x 1   = _____

Miles of bus travel   _____ x .018 = _____

Miles of train travel   _____ x .013 = _____

Total dollars spent annually [for goods, services,
mortgage and car payments, tuition, travel, etc., but not
including contributions to charity]   _____ x .03 = _____

TOTAL GALLONS [in gasoline equivalents]   _____

Goal for next year   _____

How to get there:

Serve God, Save the Planet Energy Audit[10]

Use your most recent electricity and fuel bills to estimate the following:

Annual kWh of electricity	12,430	x .06	=	740
Annual therms or ccf of natural gas		x .88	=	
Annual gallons of #2 fuel oil	800	x 1.23	=	984
Annual gallons of propane	120	x .80	=	96 – or –
Annual pounds of propane		x .19	=	
Annual cords of wood		x 220	=	

Car 1: __18,120__ divided by __24__ x 1 = __755__
miles driven annually   mpg

Car 2: __10,000__ divided by __30__ x 1 = __333__
miles driven annually   mpg

Car 3: _____ divided by _____ x 1 = _____
miles driven annually   mpg

Diesel vehicle:

_____ divided by _____ x 1.23 = _____
miles driven annually   mpg

Miles of airline travel	6,900	x .044	=	304
Gallons of gasoline used annually for boats, mowers, snowmobiles, chainsaws, ATVs, etc.	50	x 1	=	50
Miles of bus travel		x .018	=	
Miles of train travel		x .013	=	

Total dollars spent annually [for goods, services, mortgage and car payments, tuition, travel, etc., but not including contributions to charity]   48,500   x .03   =   1,455

TOTAL GALLONS [in gasoline equivalents]   4,717
Goal for next year   4,245

How to get there:
- Change light bulbs
- Vacation close to home next year
- Carpool to work
- Hang laundry on a clothesline in the summer

Loving the forsaken

How to Care for the Disabled, Orphaned, and Incarcerated

6

"The times we find ourselves having to wait on others may be the perfect opportunities to train ourselves to wait on the Lord."[1]

— Joni Eareckson Tada, founder, Joni & Friends ministry

start⟩ Group Interaction

> Get Connected

1 minute

Have someone in the group read aloud this brief description of the session theme.

Amid busy lives that yield jam-packed days, it is easy to focus only on your own tasks, troubles, needs, and plans. Session 6 invites you to look at the world from a vastly different vantage point — through the eyes of "unloved others."

God calls his followers to represent Jesus Christ not just to people who look the same, act the same, talk the same, and vote the same way that you do, but to *every* man and *every* woman who needs his care. Your actions matter. Your choices matter. Choose today to **start>**.

"Religion that God our Father accepts as pure and faultless is this: to look after orphans and widows in their distress and to keep oneself from being polluted by the world."

—James 1:27

> Know Your Neighbor   2 minutes

Using one or two words, share your current beliefs or assumptions about the session theme.

What does it mean to be "disenfranchised"?

> Give Your Heart and Mind to God   1 minute

It sometimes seems easier to consider those who are widowed, orphaned, and incarcerated as "categories" instead of as the crown of all creation, but those who love God are called to adopt an altogether different mind-set. As you prepare to work through session 6, ask him for eyes that are open so that you see suffering people as God sees them, for ears that hear clearly the stories that break God's heart, and for arms that will stretch themselves toward embracing people as Jesus Christ did when he walked upon the earth. At some point every Christ-follower was in need of adoption, tenderness, and release from bondage. Remember how you felt then, and let God use that empathy for good during this session.

> Learn Together   30 minutes

If you'd like to take a few notes as you watch the session 6 video segment, use the space below.

> Discuss "Loving the Forsaken" 15 minutes

You may not have time to discuss all of the questions in this section — that's okay! Cover as many as you can, thoughtfully, thoroughly, and with great attentiveness.

1. Session teacher Jim Cymbala said that the "only advertisement for Christ on this earth is we Christians — the body of Christ, the church of the Lord." What do you want for that "billboard" to communicate to the watching world? Note your answer on the sign below and then share what you wrote with your small group.

Now craft a second slogan on the billboard below that reflects what you think the *watching world* sees when they "read" Christ-followers' lives.

As it relates to those who are disenfranchised among you, why do you suppose there is disparity at times between what Christians *wish* their billboards said and what the watching world *actually* sees? Discuss your thoughts with the entire group, noting on the lines below the ideas you hear that resonate with you most.

_____

_____

_____

_____

_____

_____

2. In the video segment, Jim Cymbala said, "The greatest expression of love is to reach out to those who are soiled and unworthy and to lift them up with love." Think about a time when God himself reached out to you along the way and lifted you up with love. Describe the experience in the space below before sharing it with your group.

What is your most recent memory of another *person* "lifting you up" with love? Jot down the recollection below, and if time permits, discuss with your group why the rescue was so meaningful to you.

3. Host John Ortberg closed this session with the reminder that all of us at one time were imprisoned, orphaned, and alone. What fears, inhibitions, or insecurities might keep Christ-followers from reaching out to those who find themselves imprisoned, orphaned, or alone and crave to be "lifted up" today? Perhaps it's the fear of compromising personal safety, or an insecurity about knowing what words to say. Log your group's input below, checking the box beside the entry or entries you'd most like to overcome in your own life.

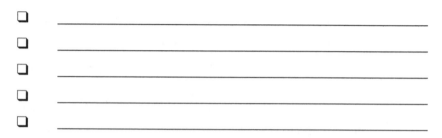

Chuck Colson made the statement, "Culture is merely a reflection of our beliefs; culture is religion incarnate. You want to change the culture — the world — you must change the church." As you conclude your group time, briefly consider the fact that one of the first steps that must be taken in order to "change the church" is to change the way we as individuals relate to people *outside* the church. In other words, we must get better about engaging in other people's stories.

It is far easier to reach out to someone, to be the love of Christ in their lives, when you know their story. You'll be given an opportunity to go discover other people's stories in a moment, but for now, consider your *own* story as you move into the "Now Is the Time" activity for this session.

> Now Is the Time

This is the most important part of the session — how your small group will put faith into action. Make each other accountable for starting today!

In 2006 at their annual Leadership Summit, an exercise called "Cardboard Testimonies" was debuted globally at Willow Creek Community Church.[2] Men and women from a variety of backgrounds told their life stories in two phrases — statements that reflected who they were before they knew Christ and who they have become since then. As the three examples below show, one woman was "going downhill fast and hit bottom alone" until Jesus took her hand at age twenty-four. A man who had been "addicted to cocaine for twenty years" found that, through Jesus, his desire for drugs was taken away. Another had been "lost" until, through Christ, he was "found."

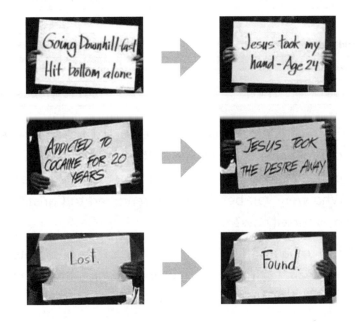

Dozens of other cardboard testimonies followed, including the before-and-after phrases you see on page 126. Scan the grid, circling any testimonies that seem to resemble aspects of your personal spiritual journey.

Who I Was Before I Knew Christ ...	Who I've Become Since ...
Angry Thief	Peaceful Man Who Knows He Was Bought with a Price
Clinically Depressed in 2006	Soaring on Wings of Eagles, 2009
Homeless and Afraid	At Home in My God and My Church
Foster Child without a Family	Adopted into the Family of God
Baseball Was My God	God Is My God Forever
Darkness	Light in the Lord
Nearly Lost Baby When Five Months Pregnant	She Turns Two Tomorrow
Had a Hole in My Heart	Discovered It Was God I Was Missing
Gripped by Destructive Behavior	Set Free by the Love of Christ
Abused as a Child and Angry	Cared for by My Heavenly Father
Five Miscarriages	Seven Adopted Orphans
Held Captive by Porn	Released into God's Real Purpose for Me
Fear and Doubt	Peace
Lost and Wounded Sheep	Lifted Up by a Very Good Shepherd

When you are vulnerable enough to embrace and acknowledge your own areas of brokenness, you will be better able to help meet others in their place of need. In that spirit, consider your own "before-and-after" story of faith: Who were you before you surrendered to Christ? How would you describe yourself now?

First, turn to pages 141 – 142 and take a couple of minutes to create your own cardboard testimony. Once your entire group has completed the exercise, share your "before-and-after" with them.

Next, in the coming days, discover the "cardboard testimonies" of two or three people you don't know by going on a "Story Hunt." (See pages 143 –146.) Pose a few of the questions from the questionnaire in an attempt to learn their stories and gain insight into their hearts. And as you practice embracing men and women the way God himself longs to embrace them, see how your heavenly Father might open your heart to helping oppressed and outcast people right at their point of need.

> Close with Prayer 1 minute

The end of this time together is really the beginning of enormous Good Samaritan possibility for you and your group. Take a moment to offer a prayer of thanksgiving and commitment to God, such as the one that follows.

> *O Lord, the hard-won miles*
> *Have worn my stumbling feet:*
> *Oh, soothe me with thy smiles,*
> *And make my life complete.*
> *The thorns were thick and keen*
> *Where'er I trembling trod;*
> *The way was long between*
> *My wounded feet and God.*
> *Where healing waters flow*
> *Do thou my footsteps lead.*
> *My heart is aching so;*
> *Thy gracious balm I need.*

— Paul Laurence Dunbar, the son of ex-slaves and the first African American to gain widespread fame as a poet; written in 1906 as a personal retrospection, just before his death from tuberculosis

start》 *Personal Reflection*

Living out your faith in real and tangible ways is more than just a six-week curriculum — it is a lifelong journey. The "Personal Reflection" section is your "diary" and "guide" as you go forward on this quest. Of course, like any journey, this one will be easier and more fruitful with the support and encouragement of others. **JustStart.org** *is that community. There you'll find other stories and testimonies just like yours, links to organizations and people who need your help and special skills, and opportunities to Learn, Live, and Lead a Good Samaritan lifestyle.*

To reconnect with this session's topic as you dive into the three-part "On Your Own" section, answer the questions below, which reference the DVD material you viewed during your small group time.

1   **2**   **3**

1. **Jim Cymbala** said that when he thinks of all the love that God has shown him, despite his many fumblings and failings, it becomes even more important to show love to others. What attitudes or actions are stirred in you when you consider the love that God has shown you? Record your thoughts below.

2. **Philippa Lei** drew attention to the fact that because there is so much need in the world, she can often feel overwhelmed, wondering, "Where do I start?" To help her overcome those feelings, she tries to remember that even small contributions can make a huge difference in God's economy. What is an example of a small action or

deed someone has done on your behalf that has yielded big results in your life?

3. **Chuck Colson** said, "It is a blessing to give of ourselves, and to see how God uses us to bless other people in our lives." When was the last time you experienced the blessing of blessing another person's life? Describe how the event impacted you.

How might God want to use that experience as motivation for you to continue being a blessing in others' lives?

❯ **On Your Own** | START LEARNING

Since its inception in 1999, Church Under the Bridge[3] in Waco, Texas, has welcomed those who are marginalized in society. The church's pastor, Jimmy Dorrell, explains their founding rationale in the excerpts below. After reading his comments, respond to the questions that follow.

Believing that God blesses his church with the least of these sisters and brothers, acceptance [of them by our church] has been normative. Persons with mental retardation, mental illness, physical disabilities, and emotional or developmental challenges are embraced as valuable people....

Of all organizations on the earth, the church should be the most inclusive one. Jesus made it so. Going into the highways and the byways, he invited the tax collector, the prostitute, the leper, the beggar, the widow, the sick, the criminal, and the formerly demon-possessed into the kingdom of God. Based only on the affirmation of his lord-ship and a repentant heart, those the status quo of society often rejects are the very ones who become kingdom representatives....

Immediately, we pull back from embracing this view because of the challenges it brings. The marginalized bring discomfort to our otherwise sterile environment. They often look, smell, and act differently [than we do], creating discomfort and unease. They can intrude on our organized liturgies, speaking too loudly or inappropriately. They may project nonverbal messages through grimaces or stares that threaten us. Their body odor may infringe on our olfactory comfort and distract us. They may even use language deemed vulgar or rude that offends those with rules of proper talk and mannerisms. Though rarely sought, it is this intrusive discomfort that often provides the greatest opportunity to spiritually mature.[4]

Pastor Dorrell says that, "Persons with mental retardation, mental illness, physical disabilities, and emotional or developmental challenges are ... valuable people." In your estimation, what qualities make a person "valuable"? Note your insights below.

Why might God choose marginalized and imperfect people to become "kingdom representatives" of his perfect and glorious work?

When have you seen God use the "intrusive discomfort" Dorrell mentions to develop spiritual maturity in you?

First John 3:17 – 18 says, "If anyone has material possessions and sees a brother or sister in need but has no pity on them, how can the love of God be in you? Dear children, let us not love with words or tongue but with actions and in truth." What emotions bubble to the surface in your mind and heart as you think about God's call to reach out to people who are broken and obviously in need? Check the boxes beside any items from the following list that apply.

❑ Anticipation ❑ Eagerness

❑ Apprehension ❑ Enthusiasm

❑ Anxiety ❑ Excitement

❑ Concern ❑ Fear

❑ Curiosity ❑ Frustration

❑ Denial ❑ Joy

❑ Despair ❑ Passion

Based on the emotions you selected, what would you like to convey to God before you move on? Jot down your thoughts in the form of a prayer on the lines below.

_____

_____

_____

_____

With that plea to God in mind, which "Learn" opportunity from the list on page 132 might be an appropriate way for you to begin caring more deeply for people who are disenfranchised in the world around you? Ask God to expand your heart's capacity for loving others as you endeavor to achieve it.

LEARN ●○○

● **Read of ragamuffins.** Read the excerpt from Brennan Manning's *The Ragamuffin Gospel* found on page 147 and note your thoughts on what it means to love others as God loves them in the Journal section of this guide.

● **Gather up hope.** Watch stories of transformation from around the globe, produced by Prison Fellowship International (pfi.org/films). As you view the film(s), pay special attention to how God might want to use *you* as an agent of hope and transformation in this generation.

● **Take note of paths you've crossed.** For one day, make a list of every person with whom you cross paths, including the friend you met for lunch as well as the person panhandling on the street. Whether you know their names or not, whether you engaged them in conversation or not, write down what you saw about their situation, as well as what you imagine God saw. Which of the people you remember would you consider your "neighbor"? Which are not? Record your thoughts and recollections in the Journal section.

● **Let courage have its way.** Read the Serenity Prayer aloud (see below). Spend a few minutes in prayer, asking God for insight as to what changes in the world around you he would have you make, and then for the courage to make them.

The Serenity Prayer

*God, grant me the serenity
to accept the things I cannot change;
the courage to change the things I can;
and the wisdom to know the difference.*

*Living one day at a time;
enjoying one moment at a time;
accepting hardships as the pathway to peace;
taking as He did, this sinful world
as it is, not as I would have it;
trusting that He will make all things right
if I surrender to His Will;
that I may be reasonably happy in this life
and supremely happy with Him
forever in the next.
Amen.*[5]

—Reinhold Niebuhr

> **On Your Own** | START LIVING IT OUT

Pastor Jim Cymbala referenced a powerful part of King David's story that is found in 2 Samuel. A man named Mephibosheth, who had been crippled since age five, was invited to come and dine at the table of the king. Read 2 Samuel 9:6 – 11. Then answer the questions below.

When is the last time you felt like Mephibosheth must have felt that day, completely unworthy of the kindness of another and yet so grateful to be welcomed into the warmth of community? Describe the experience in the space below.

In Luke 14:13 Jesus says, "But when you give a banquet, invite the poor, the crippled, the lame, the blind," which is exactly what King David did when he welcomed an alienated outcast named Mephibosheth to dine at his table. As you consider your life today, who is seated at *your* table, figuratively speaking? Those who are beautiful and well-adjusted, or those who have been crippled and outcast, ones who feel humbled by your care? Only Republicans or Democrats? Only people your age or race? Only those whose income matches yours? Only those who have something to give you in return? Or those who look and act and spend and vote quite differently from you?

For each of the "seats" pictured in the diagram on page 134, jot down the names or descriptions of a few people in your life whom God might be calling you to enfold in community. Perhaps it's an overly chatty neighbor. Maybe it's a colleague who grew up in foster care. It could be that waiter at your favorite restaurant whom you know once served time. It may be the postal carrier you've never stopped to engage in conversation. You'll be given an opportunity to cross paths with these "spiritual Mephibosheths" a bit later; for now, simply log the ones God brings to mind.

Jim Cymbala said that too often, we want for Jesus to "clean the fish before we're willing to catch them," but clearly that wasn't King David's approach. How would your journey toward placing your faith in Christ have looked differently if God had made you "clean up your act" prior to coming to him? Note your answer in the space below.

What aspects of Christ's character might you experience when you accept the world's "dirty fish" instead of demanding that they be made clean before you embrace them? Complete the grid on the next page. An example has been provided for you.

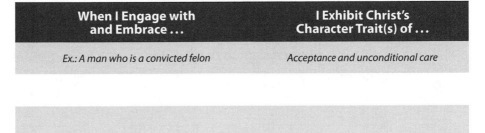

When I Engage with and Embrace ...	I Exhibit Christ's Character Trait(s) of ...
Ex.: A man who is a convicted felon	*Acceptance and unconditional care*

How are you feeling about the possibility of welcoming a few of your "spiritual Mephibosheths" into your life? Pause for a few minutes as you consider that question. Then, in the space below, tell God the truth about the themes running through your head and your heart at this point, noting your areas of weakness, your various fears, and your points of confusion.

God, I'm feeling ...

Please replace these areas of weakness with your strength ...

these fears with your confidence ...

and these points of confusion with your wisdom ...

Spend as much time in prayer as it takes for God's strength, confidence, and wisdom to flood your thoughts. Close your time by asking him to give you an open door to reach out to one of your spiritual Mephibosheths today.

CHECKING IN

As you move into the selection of your "Live It Out" action item for this session, reflect back on the cardboard testimony you crafted during the "Now Is the Time" section. Remember your before-and-after phrases from pages 141–142? Note them on the lines below.

Before I met Christ, I was _____

Since then, I've become _____

Keep in mind the joy of your own journey, as well as the power of learning another person's story and honoring what God may be up to in his or her life, as you select and engage in one of the action items below.

LIVE IT OUT

● **Deliver meals on wheels.** Those who are homebound or hospitalized love to see a friendly smile. Browse mowaa.org and consider locating a local program this week.

● **Turn gossip into action.** What you chatter about might just reveal how you could get involved. Next time you find yourself sermonizing to your spouse after reading the morning's headlines or after you get off the phone with a friend, stop and ask God, "Is this where I'm supposed to serve?"

● **Protect a child.** Become a Child Crisis Partner through World Vision. Millions of children worldwide desperately need help. These children live a nightmare, facing issues such as abuse, exploitation, forced labor, rape, and abandonment. For $20 a month, you can help one child after another escape a life of horror. To learn more, visit worldvision.org.

● **Look like Luke 16:10.** God desires that you use your resources to advance *his* kingdom rather than your own. Commit a portion of your funds to someone in need this week. Prove to God that you can be trusted in the little hidden things so that someday you will be trusted with much.

● **En-franchise someone today.** Commit one action this week to begin helping *"en-franchise"* someone who craves care. Speak a word, pray a prayer, write a letter, visit an inmate, wrap loving arms around a fatherless child — whatever your action, thank God for your newfound capacity to care.

● **Commit to pray.** This very day many men and women are reintegrating into the community after being discharged from treatment facilities or released from prison. Whether immigrants, homeless, refugees, undocumented workers, illiterate, or different from you in some other way, carry them to the throne of God in prayer. Invite the Spirit to soften your heart toward others and to see them as children of God, created in God's image.

● **Offer pro bono work.** Reflect the mercy and love of Christ by providing free services such as counseling, legal work, carpentry, babysitting, cooking/nutrition classes, parenting skills, ride sharing, literacy classes, art and music lessons; visiting those who are homebound or hospitalized; assisting with procuring identification, and so forth. Your expertise likely is just what someone needs today!

● **Shoot hoops for good.** Join thousands of participants and teams from around the world shooting free throws to benefit children orphaned by AIDS in Africa. For details on "Hoops for Hope," visit worldvision.org/start.

❯ **On Your Own**|START LEADING

Margery Williams wrote a children's book in the early 1920s titled, *The Velveteen Rabbit*. As the story goes, one Christmas a young boy received a stuffed velveteen rabbit, which was quickly snubbed by the boy's other more expensive, more impressive toys.

One day while chatting with the boy's toy horse, the Velveteen Rabbit learns that if a toy is really and truly loved, it will become real. Soon enough, the Velveteen Rabbit becomes the boy's favorite companion, but even as the rabbit becomes shabbier, the boy's love for it never wanes. In the woods near the boy's home, the Velveteen Rabbit meets actual rabbits and discovers the differences between him and them. They can hop, but he cannot. They can jump, but he cannot. They can shed real fur, but alas, he cannot.

The Velveteen Rabbit remains faithfully by the boy's side until one day when the boy falls ill with scarlet fever. Sadly, the boy is too sick to play for quite some time. When he finally recovers, his doctor instructs him to visit the seaside in order to heal completely. Of course the boy wishes to take the Velveteen Rabbit along, but his doctor won't allow it. He must burn his favorite companion along with all his other germ-laden toys, the doctor advises, to avoid becoming re-infected with the disease.

The boy is gifted with a brand new stuffed rabbit — this time a plush one with glass eyes. He is so excited to be headed to the seaside that he forgets all about his old Velveteen Rabbit.

While the Rabbit awaits his fate beside the bonfire one day, a real tear falls from his eye. Suddenly, the Nursery Magic Fairy appears and tells the Rabbit that he indeed was loved by the boy. The Velveteen Rabbit is delivered to the forest, where he hops and jumps alongside all the other real rabbits the rest of the days of his life.[6]

> Whether this is your first time hearing the story of the Velveteen Rabbit or it was your favorite book as a child, what similarities do you see between the messages in Margery Williams' book and the message of this session?

> In the biblical parable, the Good Samaritan provided intentional and thorough care, but it was temporary care at best. Perhaps God has you in mind for a similar short-term assignment. If you knew that your care — even temporary care — could "give life" to someone this week, how would it change your attitudes, your actions, and the way you approach your role in embracing the disenfranchised in the world?

> As you wrap up the "On Your Own" portion of this session, read through the six "Lead" action items that follow. See which item makes your heart beat faster and commit to God that you'll give that one a try this week.

LEAD   ○○●

● **Book worms, unite!** Facilitate a book club that dives into books such as *Hunger for Healing, Trolls and Truth,* or *Same Kind of Different as Me* to continue to cultivate understanding of your own brokenness and a deeper level of compassion toward others.

● **Become a pen pal.** Form a team of pen pals within your small group or larger faith community. Choose a group of people who might need an extra dose of hope and encouragement, such as the men, women, and children supported by the efforts of Buckner International (bucknerinternational.org); or sponsor a child through World Vision (worldvision.org). Then write to them on a monthly basis.

● **Let your experience shine.** Organize a tutoring group/ministry that will assist people in preparing for the GED exam or to learn basic professional skills such as typing and resume writing.

● **Rally the night owls.** Find out when men and women will be discharged from the county or city jail in your area and organize a team of people to meet them with food; resources to assist them in finding practical help such as meals, shelter, and employment; and open arms. Most adults are released between midnight and three a.m. and without immediately available resources. Have card-sized maps available to show freshly freed people where they may find shelter, case management, and a meal the following morning. Better yet, allow them to sleep one night in your church gym and then transport them the next day to an outreach center with which you have developed a partnership.

● **Take it one step at a time.** If you are in recovery, give others a hand up by starting a Twelve Step group at your church or in your community.

● **Include the excluded.** Invite men and women from area shelters and treatment centers to a dinner/dance that is hosted by your faith community. (Often, to comply with policies and safety parameters, these agencies will provide staff to chaperone.) Make everyone feel welcomed, offer a small token of your appreciation while they're there, and thank them with kind words and a hug as they leave.

start > *Ready for More?*

> Read

- *You Were Made for More: The Life You Have, the Life God Wants You to Have*, Jim Cymbala (Zondervan)

- *When God Weeps: Why Our Sufferings Matter to the Almighty*, Joni Eareckson Tada (Zondervan)

- *How Now Shall We Live?*, Charles Colson (Tyndale)

- *Your Journey with Jesus*, Ron Nikkel (Christian Focus)

- *Trolls and Truth: 14 Realities about Today's Church That We Don't Want to See*, Jimmy Dorrell (New Hope)

> Surf

- juststart.org

- pfi.org (Prison Fellowship International)

- theprisonyard.org

- joniandfriends.org

- kairosprisonministry.org

Cardboard Testimony

Who I was before I knew Christ . . .

Cardboard Testimony

Who I've been becoming since . . .

Story Hunt

In the coming days, use the grids on the following three pages to "interview" a few people whom you've never met. Find out their names, their backgrounds, and as much about their journeys as they're willing to share. Sample questions follow, but let the Spirit of God lead you as you embark on each conversation. When you return to this guide afterward, jot down as much of the exchange as you can recall before writing down a prayer on behalf of each person you met.

Story Hunt

Name:

Where They've Come From ...

Geographically *["Where did you grow up? Where have you lived/traveled? What's your favorite type of environment?"]*

Occupationally *["What did you want to be when you grew up? What type of work do you most enjoy doing?"]*

Recreationally *["Did you enjoy sports as a kid? In an ideal world, what would your 'perfect' day involve?"]*

Relationally *["Who has had the greatest impact on your life? If you could spend an hour with anyone, who would it be?"]*

Emotionally *["What are a few of your favorite moments from life so far? What about your lowest lows?"]*

Spiritually *["Has there ever been a spiritual component to your life? How have you sensed God at work in your life so far?"]*

Where They Are Today ...

["What's an average day like for you now? If you could change one thing about your life, what would it be?"]

Notes/Learnings from Our Discussion

My Prayer on Their Behalf

Story Hunt

Name:

Where They've Come From …

Geographically *["Where did you grow up? Where have you lived/traveled? What's your favorite type of environment?"]*

Occupationally *["What did you want to be when you grew up? What type of work do you most enjoy doing?"]*

Recreationally *["Did you enjoy sports as a kid? In an ideal world, what would your 'perfect' day involve?"]*

Relationally *["Who has had the greatest impact on your life? If you could spend an hour with anyone, who would it be?"]*

Emotionally *["What are a few of your favorite moments from life so far? What about your lowest lows?"]*

Spiritually *["Has there ever been a spiritual component to your life? How have you sensed God at work in your life so far?"]*

Where They Are Today …

["What's an average day like for you now? If you could change one thing about your life, what would it be?"]

Notes/Learnings from Our Discussion

My Prayer on Their Behalf

Story Hunt

Name:

Where They've Come From ...

Geographically *["Where did you grow up? Where have you lived/traveled? What's your favorite type of environment?"]*

Occupationally *["What did you want to be when you grew up? What type of work do you most enjoy doing?"]*

Recreationally *["Did you enjoy sports as a kid? In an ideal world, what would your 'perfect' day involve?"]*

Relationally *["Who has had the greatest impact on your life? If you could spend an hour with anyone, who would it be?"]*

Emotionally *["What are a few of your favorite moments from life so far? What about your lowest lows?"]*

Spiritually *["Has there ever been a spiritual component to your life? How have you sensed God at work in your life so far?"]*

Where They Are Today ...

["What's an average day like for you now? If you could change one thing about your life, what would it be?"]

Notes/Learnings from Our Discussion

My Prayer on Their Behalf

Excerpt from *The Ragamuffin Gospel*

by Brennan Manning

Jesus spent a disproportionate amount of time with people described in the gospels as the poor, the blind, the lame, the lepers, the hungry, sinners, prostitutes, tax collectors, the persecuted, the downtrodden, the captives, those possessed by unclean spirits, all who labor and are heavy burdened, the rabble who know nothing of the law, the crowds, the little ones, the least, the last, and the lost sheep of the house of Israel. In short, Jesus hung out with ragamuffins. He related with warmth and compassion to the middle and upper classes not because of their family connections, financial clout, intelligence, or Social Register status but because they, too, were God's children.

In his reply to the disciples' question about who is the greatest in the Kingdom of heaven (Matthew 18:1), Jesus abolished any distinction between the elite and the ordinary in the Christian community. "He called a little child to him and set the child in front of them. Then he said, 'I tell you solemnly, unless you change and become like little children, you will never enter the kingdom of heaven. And so, the one who makes himself as little as this little child is the greatest in the kingdom of heaven'" (Matthew 18:2 – 4).

Jesus cuts to the heart of the matter as he sits the child on his knee. The child is unself-conscious, incapable of pretense. I am reminded of the night little John Dyer, three years old, knocked on our door flanked by his parents. I looked down and said, "Hi, John. I am delighted to see you." He looked neither to the right nor left. His face was set like flint. He narrowed his eyes with the apocalyptic glint of an aimed gun. "Where's the cookies?" he demanded.

The Kingdom belongs to people who aren't trying to look good or impress anybody, even themselves. They are not plotting how they can call attention to themselves, worrying about how their actions will be interpreted or wondering if they will get gold stars for their behavior. Twenty centuries later, Jesus speaks pointedly to the preening ascetic trapped in the fatal narcissism of spiritual perfectionism, to those of us caught up in boasting about our victories in the vineyard, to those of us fretting and flapping about our human weaknesses and character defects. The child doesn't have to struggle to get himself in a good position for having a relationship with God; he doesn't have to craft ingenious ways of explaining his position to Jesus; he doesn't have to create a pretty face for himself; he doesn't have to achieve any state of spiritual feeling or intellectual understanding. All he has to do is happily accept the cookies: the gift of the Kingdom.[7]

Journal

Journal

Journal

Journal

Journal

Journal

Notes

Foreword: People of the Possible and a Gospel Devoid of Holes

1. Paraphrased from Rich Stearns, *The Hole in Our Gospel* (Nashville: Thomas Nelson, 2009).

Session 1: Becoming a Good Samaritan

1. Jeffrey Sachs, "The Obama Generation Takes the Helm," *GOOD*, January/February 2009, 16.

Session 2: Caring for the Sick

1. www.thinkexist.com/quotations.
2. www.aidsresponsibility.org.
3. *UN AIDS Report on the Global AIDS Epidemic*, 2008.
4. *The aWAKE Project: Uniting Against the African AIDS Crisis*, second edition (Nashville: W Publishing Group, 2002), 219–221.
5. From Dr. Peter Moore, *The Little Book of Pandemics* (London: Elwin Street Limited, 2007), 57–59, 67, 69, 81, 83, 124–125.
6. Thomas Fuller, *Gnomologia*, 1732.
7. Bono, *On the Move* (Nashville: W Publishing Group, 2006), 57.
8. *GOOD*, January/February 2009: 34.

Session 3: Seeking Justice and Reconciliation

1. Lydia Bean, "Bridging the Great Divide," *Sojourners*, March 2009: 23–24.
2. www.martinlutherkingjrdayeveryday.com.
3. http://blog.sojo.net/2009/02/23/10-reasons-we-dont-like-to-talk-about-race/.

Session 4: Honoring the Poor

1. Bryant Myers, *Walking with the Poor: Principles and Practices of Transformational Development* (New York: Orbis Books, 2005), 57.

2. http://www.familycare.org/news/if_the_world.htm.

3. Matthew Parris, *Times Online*, 27 December 2008. www.timesonline.co.uk.

4. Mike Yankoski, *Under the Overpass* (Colorado Springs: WaterBrook/Multnomah, 2005), 14 – 16.

5. National Curriculum and Training Institute, Inc.® NCTI, revised 2005, © 1994, www.ncti.org.

Session 5: Tending to God's Creation

1. Thomas Kostigen, *You are Here: Exposing the Vital Link between What We Do and What That Does to Our Planet* (San Francisco: Harper One, 2008), 15.

2. http://www.faithandworship.com/creation_prayers.htm.

3. *Green Guide* (Washington, D.C.: National Geographic Society, 2008), 96.

4. Kostigen, 126.

5. Philippe Bourseiller, *365 Ways to Save the Earth: New and Updated Edition* (New York: Abrams, 2008), February 3 entry.

6. Kostigen, 159.

7. Matthew Sleeth, *Serve God, Save the Planet* (Grand Rapids, Mich.: Zondervan, 2006), 93.

8. Based on author interview with Mary Margaret Bartley, 2009. Used with permission.

9. Used with permission, Matthew Sleeth, blessedearth.org.

10. Ibid.

Session 6: Loving the Forsaken

1. www.dailychristianquote.com.

2. The content and photos included here are used with permission of the Willow Creek Association.

3. churchunderthebridge.org.

4. Jimmy Dorrell, *Trolls and Truth: 14 Realities about Today's Church that We Don't Want to See* (Birmingham, Ala.: New Hope Publishers, 2006), 71, 76, 80.

5. www.aahistory.com.

6. Author's summary of Margery Williams' *The Velveteen Rabbit: Or, How Toys Become Real* (New York: Doubleday, 1922).

7. Brennan Manning, *The Ragamuffin Gospel* (Sisters, Oreg.: Multnomah Books, 1990), 49 – 51.

the **end**
of **poverty**
starts with her

Want to help end global poverty? Recent studies have shown that the most effective way to overcome poverty is to strengthen the girls and women it affects.

Yet many girls in developing countries may never see the inside of a classroom, receive quality health care, or be able to provide enough food for their own children.

You can change that.

There are **thousands** of girls waiting right now for a compassionate sponsor like you. Show one of them God's love by helping her access things like clean water, better nutrition, health care, education, and economic opportunities – benefits that will extend to her family, her community, and other children in need.

Start changing a child's life today. To find out how you can sponsor a child, visit www.worldvision.org/start or call 1-888-465-6835.

World Vision is a Christian humanitarian organization dedicated to helping children, families, and their communities worldwide reach their full potential by tackling the causes of poverty and injustice.

Share Your Thoughts

With the Author: Your comments will be forwarded to the author when you send them to *zauthor@zondervan.com*.

With Zondervan: Submit your review of this book by writing to *zreview@zondervan.com*.

Free Online Resources at
www.zondervan.com

Zondervan AuthorTracker: Be notified whenever your favorite authors publish new books, go on tour, or post an update about what's happening in their lives at www.zondervan.com/authortracker.

Daily Bible Verses and Devotions: Enrich your life with daily Bible verses or devotions that help you start every morning focused on God. Visit www.zondervan.com/newsletters.

Free Email Publications: Sign up for newsletters on Christian living, academic resources, church ministry, fiction, children's resources, and more. Visit www.zondervan.com/newsletters.

Zondervan Bible Search: Find and compare Bible passages in a variety of translations at www.zondervanbiblesearch.com.

Other Benefits: Register yourself to receive online benefits like coupons and special offers, or to participate in research.

ZONDERVAN®

ZONDERVAN.com/
AUTHORTRACKER
follow your favorite authors